Cybele, with Bluebonnets

Charles L. Harness

Edited by Priscilla Olson

For Colleen

Charles L. Harness

The NESFA Press
Post Office Box 809
Framingham, MA 01701
2002

FIRST EDITION
July 2002

International Standard Book Number:
1-886778-41-8

Cybele, with Bluebonnets

In Search of Bluebonnets

This book came to NESFA in a roundabout and ultimately satisfying way.

It's a very unusual book for us to do, too.

It's a book for chemists who might appreciate magical realism—though that barely describes the power and passion of the material.

Like many other works by Charles Harness, it's about loss and gain. Mostly, however, it's about love.

It's about love for a woman, but also for a lost time and place. It's about a man looking at his life and beliefs, and reaching for those things that made them matter.

Reaching ever backwards for the elusive scent of bluebonnets . . .

Priscilla Olson

INTRODUCTION

The best way to introduce this new novel by the legendary Charles L. Harness is to start with Gene Wolfe's words to the publisher:

"There are perhaps a thousand wonderful books. Most of us are fortunate if we so much as hear the titles of them in the course of a lifetime. Very few of us ever touch the covers of more than half a dozen. This is one of them. If you do not buy the copy you are holding, you are not likely to see one again."

All of Harness's novels flow from the wellsprings of autobiography. Remembrance refracted through a science-informed imagination is what gives his novels reality and conviction. The author can't help it; his talent works by occupying his created worlds with authentic experience and knowledge, however fanciful his conceptions.

When J. G. Ballard published *Empire of the Sun,* his autobiographical novel about his boyhood internment by the Japanese during the Second World War, it was clear that this novel was perhaps a key to all his science fiction and later novels, in which we find the signs, footprints, and healed wounds of the past. With Charles L. Harness we also sense bits of autobiography in his fictions, which may also include dreams and what-might-have-beens from his life, transformed into artful alternate realities.

But where in previous novels the autobiographical details lend an extra emotional charge to the fantastic dramas, and need no further explanation, the story of *Cybele* is more overtly autobiographical, in the manner of the growing-up novel. It is full of painful joys and beauties, as well as tragedies, and a sense of youthful places. The novel explains itself, but one feels that the author was more willing to approach his secret places and the hidden center with greater courage. I'm reminded of C. M. Kornbluth's comment that the major component of fiction, especially science fiction and fantasy, is more concerned with "unconscious symbolic material," with "the individual's relationship to his family

9

and the raw universe than with the individual's relationship to society." Social criticism is implicit, because a human being is presented from "inside" his experience. What else the reader sees in the wider context is up to him.

Cybele is not a long novel, and it keeps intently to the details the author wishes to present. What most interests him affects us more deeply because of this intense focus which sets all else aside.

It might be described as a ghost story, even a tall ghost story, in which the teller, Joe Barnes, knows full well how much he may be fooling himself and the reader in describing the miraculous, perhaps supernatural, events that guide his life. Or they may be naturally occurring phenomena poorly observed and only fancifully explained. This first love of the teller's life, Cybele, has an undoubted effect on his life, whatever the explanations of how this comes about, and that is the larger truth of the story. The past and its people do live on in all of us. They may do so because we keep them with us, or because it can't be helped. There is survival after death, in this way.

The denial of death and the power of hope are major themes in Harness's work, clearly present in his classic novel *The Paradox Men,* which I had the privilege of shepherding back into print three times. In that novel Alar the Thief is also a ghost of himself, bringing an active hope back to humanity, as Ulysses did when he came home and set his house in order. Ghost stories are perhaps the classic form of storytelling, because storytelling is itself a way of resurrecting the dead past. Once we began to think of death as an observed finality, we also began to wonder whether what we see in the physical ruin of a human being is the last word, and to wish that it might be otherwise. It's not over, ever, is a grand cry, and a powerful hope. A ghost story attempts to redeem a loss by making a "return" part of the story, in itself already a re-creation. One day perhaps we'll make it so, by another road—along the way of knowledge and its creative applications. Until then we have writing and poetry, and all the arts that live by remembrance, which includes being mindful of possible futures.

The telling of this novel is hypnotic. The various stories within stories of Texas life during the Great Depression exhibit a humane curiosity about the people who were part of the teller's life, despite the sharp, often bloodied edges of their behavior. Harness makes us care deeply about what happens to his people. The sense of detail, both suggested and presented, is extraordinary, as is the Twain-like ease of telling—so convincing that we accept everything we are told and believe it's so, because it is so within us.

Science, especially chemistry, plays a large role in Joe Barnes's life. He knows how to think, except when love mercifully clouds his skepticism— all to the better. He is skeptical of coincidences, but faces up to their reality.

For those of us who have read Harness, this novel can only confirm to us what we all know: that at the heart of all his works, both personal and literary, there lives a wonderful human being, whose eager, questing response to his own humanity and to the raw universe has earned him high praise for sharing his visions with his readers. Perhaps this novel will reveal him to be the major American writer whom we read in the words. His modesty prevents him from thinking of his work in this way, even though I suspect and hope that he has some inkling of his true accomplishments. He actually doesn't need to think of himself in this way; he has spent his time on the writing, which fulfills itself in his readers.

George Zebrowski
Delmar, New York
May 22, 2002

Miss Wilson

My first real contact with Cybele Wilson where I could daily undress her with adoring lascivious adolescent eyes, was in high school. She was my chemistry teacher.

She was well named. In ancient Phrygian mythology Cybele was the Goddess of Nature. Miss Cybele Wilson was a very special teacher and a very beautiful woman. I was sixteen, nearly seventeen, and she was not yet twenty-four. Sure, I had a crush on her. A lot of the boys did.

I had never seen a completely naked woman, but I had seen plenty of girls at the Forest Park swimming pool, and I had seen explicit pictures in art magazines. I had a fair idea of how they were put together.

Mentally, and working at top speed as soon as she walked into the classroom from the lab bay, I stripped her of lab coat, cotton print dress, slip, brassiere, teds. By the time she reached her desk she wore only her stockings and garters and low-heeled shoes. As I watched her come through that door and walk those eight steps, I knew how Keats had felt, "On first looking into Chapman's Homer."

She had green eyes and long light brown hair, which she gathered in a bun at the back of her head. She was of average height. If I were holding her closely, the top of her head would fit just under my chin. Her breasts were perfect, neither over-large nor undersized. They were firm, presumptively virginal, the upper surfaces sloping to the nipple.

Below her breasts came the smooth slightly rounded belly, interrupted by her navel, probably lightly touched with lint. With my hands on her opulent hips I bowed and kissed that navel. Next . . .

I had to quit. She was checking the roll and I didn't want to meet her eyes. Instantly I re-dressed her and hoped my jock strap was holding.

We sat in tiers, the highest rows in the back, so the students in the rear could see over the heads of those in the front. I sat in about the middle, out of the way, yet with a good view. Sometimes, to show us a specimen of something or other, she would leave her desk and walk up through the tiers. My heart would beat like a machine gun when she passed me. She never seemed to notice.

The year before, the student body had voted her the most popular teacher – which of course made her a bit suspect in the eyes of the administration. She was always into something new. She started an early morning volunteer class in calculus. Sadly I couldn't attend because I had an early morning paper route for the *Record-Telegram*. It netted about fifty cents a day. Money. Always money. The Great Depression was a bad time.

Not much was known about her prior life. Her origins were at least semi-local. She had been boarded and educated through high school at St. Joseph's Sanctuary, a religious institution out in the country west of the city, supported by endowments and donations. That would suggest that she was an orphan. On the other hand I understood that she had been regularly visited there by a lady who might have been her mother.

St. Joseph's had a certain bizarre claim to fame – which it neither asserted nor denied. In one of its buildings known as the Cup Chapel there was in fact a cup. And not just any cup. There were those who contended it was the very cup that Jesus drank from, at The Last Supper; which is to say, it was the Holy Grail.

It was actually on display in the Cup Chapel. You genuflected, wished for whatever miracle you had in mind, dropped your offering in the collection box, and left.

Off to one side there was a pile of discarded crutches, canes, a wheelchair, a hearing trumpet, and so on. Outrageous fakery, some said.

It was known that when Miss Wilson left St. Joseph's, she went East. From things she let drop, it appeared that she got her B.S. and M.S. from a university in Washington, D.C. And thence back home and into the august faculty of JimBowie High.

She had run-ins with the system from time to time.

Take the case of J.D. Jones.

Now of course students were not permitted to smoke in school. Some of the boys tried to get around the rule by chewing tobacco – which generated copious saliva and required frequent spitting. Hey, no problem. J.D. Jones, for example, carried a stoppered ink bottle. In chemistry he sat on the front row and we could all watch him as he went into action. As soon as Miss Wilson turned to the blackboard he'd pull out the stopper and spit. But on this particular day, with perfect timing, she walked over and confiscated his bottle. Eventually his mouth filled, and – oh boy! – he *had* to swallow. In fact, he swallowed plug and all. He turned green, and she sent him to the nurse's office. He went home for the day. His mother complained bitterly to Mr. Vachel, the principal, who called Miss Wilson into the discussion. The matter was dropped when the school nurse pointed out that nicotine in this form was a fine vermifuge and that J.D. for several years had needed a thorough worming.

Miss Wilson came out of that one smelling like a rose.

Several of the other teachers were jealous of her and suspected her of various felonies and misdemeanors, such as being an evolutionist, an atheist, or even having Yankee parents. But they were never able to prove anything.

In class she would talk about the future. "It's on the way," she would declare. "We'll have synthetic soaps. And plastics, clear as glass, tough as steel. We're going to wipe out disease with new medicines and drugs. People like Albert Einstein will show us how to split the atom. We'll have cheap new energy sources." When she got like this, her beautiful green eyes would snap and sparkle. She spoke with solemn certainty, like a beautiful Delphic priestess.

Of course, word of her weird prophecies got back to her wide circle of enemies, and they added "dangerous insanity" to her growing list of crimes.

So why did she stay? I think because she loved to teach. Teaching was her passion, the way painting was van Gogh's, or music was Beethoven's. She loved the contact of minds, the awakenings, the widened eyes when an idea registered.

My last thoughts as I fell asleep at night were generally of her. I remembered how she walked: with rhythm and meter, a lyric in classic mode. A poem by Coleridge. Even when standing totally motionless, she radiated grace. Yet it was impossible to point to any one feature that defined her beauty. It wasn't just her face (though that was beautiful). It wasn't just her body, though that was certainly superb. It was the sum total of all of her that overwhelmed me. I never tried to analyze it. It just . . . *was*.

Champ

I have to back up a few years.

A stretch of creek ran through a sort of wasteland about three miles from our home in Fort West. On the map the area is called Sycamore Park. But it isn't a park. It is owned by neither city nor county. There's no upkeep. When I was first there, aside from a few cattle wandering on the other side of barbwire fences, civilization had not yet encroached.

On this bright day of June 1925, my gang and I had gone hiking down into the park and along the creek. As usual, they went in one direction and I headed off in another.

Now, there was one particular stretch where the creek broadened into a wide flat ankle-deep mini-lake. This was my very favorite spot, because what with the long expanse of water and an abundance of flat rocks and shells along the narrow shore, I could stand barefoot in the middle of the creek bed and skip shells way up the creek.

There's a trick to making rocks skip along the water surface. I learned it by trial and error. First, the rock (or shell) must be tolerably flat. Second, it should be fairly circular. Third, it should be of a certain size, not too little, not too big, because it must be grasped neatly in the "C" formed by the curve of thumb and forefinger. Fourth, you squat low over the water, so as to give your skipper a low angle of contact. And now with all your might you simultaneously spin your missile clockwise and throw it. Your rock hits the water, bounds, hits, bounds, hits, bounds . . . maybe as many as four or five times. And finally it sinks.

Only ten-year-old boys can fully appreciate the beauties of rock skipping.

Now this particular skipper was a real show-off. It bounced *eight* times over the water, then leaped out onto the other side of the creek. Yes, I remember the feel of the serrated edges, the exact fit between thumb and forefinger: it had the look and form and shape and performance of a true champion. Right then and there I named it, Champ. It even had a black mark on it, like a "J". For me – Joe Barnes?

I decided I would keep it in a cigar box at home when it wasn't in use, or being passed around for admiration and envy. The box held various of my other treasures: a Chinese coin with a hole in it, a cannon cracker I had been saving for the day school let out (and then forgot), a poison dart I had borrowed temporarily from Mr. Mathers, my Sunday School teacher. (He had been a missionary somewhere deep in Brazil, but had caught malaria and they brought him home. Then he died, and there was no one to return it to.)

For starters I would brag about my skipper to the other boys, maybe with a demonstration. So I waded over to get it.

It had landed by a fair-sized hole in the cliffside. As I picked up my Olympian skipper, I took a close look at the hole. It had been there all along, of course, but I hadn't noticed it before, because some dead branches had mostly concealed it. But now they seemed to have fallen away.

The hole obviously led into a cave. The invitation was irresistible. I got down on my hands and knees, looked into the cave entrance, and listened.

Nothing.

Slowly, carefully, I crawled in.

Within seconds I was out again and running for my life.

As I ran, I realized I had dropped Champ inside the cave. But I wasn't going back. Not just then, anyhow. And several days later, when I *did* go back, very very cautiously, and with a flashlight, Champ was gone. Very puzzling.

During my precipitous flight upstream toward the other boys and dubious safety I tried to figure out what I had seen – or hadn't seen, and I was recalling that one of the names originally proposed for Fort West was Panther City. For all I knew, Sycamore Park was crawling with panthers.

Should I tell the gang I had probably seen a panther? As I splashed along I thought it out. No, that wouldn't work. If I mentioned the bare possibility, word would surely get back to parents, and we wouldn't be permitted to play there anymore. So I slowed down. When I rejoined them I wasn't even breathing hard.

Riverside

Granted, my fear of panthers now seems pretty silly. On the other hand, for me it was real.

Here's why.

Until I was seven we lived in Colorado City, Texas (population, then and now, 4,000). Our house was across the river from town, way off by itself, and was of course called Riverside. Dad was a country boy. He loved the solitude at Riverside, the silences. Mother was a city girl. She yearned for neighbors, noises, church activities. She wanted to live in the town; or better still, in a genuine city. And after certain things happened, she got her wish, and we moved to Fort West.

But first, about the river. The Spaniards named most of the rivers in the New World – at least those in South America and New Spain in North America. And whenever they encountered a fair size stream loaded with red clay, they called it Rio Colorado – Red River. There are two in the United States: the big one separating California and Arizona and which pours into the Gulf of California, and *my* Colorado River in Texas. And of course, there are towns on these rivers named Colorado City: one in Arizona, and *my* Colorado City, in Texas. *That's* the important one. For me, anyhow. My Colorado City is in Mitchell County, in West Texas.

My Colorado River rises mostly to the northwest, in Dawson County, as a conglomeration of streams and brooks coursing rather casually and intermittently down the escarpment of the Edwards Plateau, whence they head southeast, picking up gobs of red clay and sediments in the Permian basin, then rolling past Colorado City on towards the capital at Austin and finally emptying into the Gulf of Mexico at Matagordo (meaning Thick Bushes) between the rivers of Navidad (Christmas) and Brazos (full name, Brazos de Dios – the Arms of God). All three rivers are in fact plenty muddy and red, but since my river got named first, it got "Colorado." For tens of thousands of years all three have been doing their damndest to move the Edwards Plateau into the Gulf. This shows in the big beautiful sand bars that line the Texas coast and today help define the Inland Waterway.

Back up. I was going to tell about my encounter with a panther, and I got side-tracked, talking about the river. But it isn't all wasted. The river's where my little brother Peedo and I met the big cat.

Several times a week, after supper, Dad would announce that he was going for a little walk. At that time I was six, Peedo was three. I always asked Dad if I could go with him, and he always said no, it's too brambly, or too muddy, or something. Now, there was a big bag of cotton on the back porch, and generally, as he left, he'd stuff a wad of cotton in a trouser pocket. It was all very peculiar and mysterious, and the time had to come when I decided it was absolutely necessary to follow him and see where his walks were taking him.

So when I heard the porch door slam I knew he had his ball of cotton and was on his way. I ran to the porch, watched him disappear among the scrubby evergreens, and started out after him. And wouldn't you know it, Peedo was right behind me. "Okay," I said, "but you be quiet. You make any noise, Dad'll give us both a lickin'."

He just laughed. I took his hand. "Come on."

Five minutes into the copse, the trail vanished. We were lost. I couldn't see Dad. I stopped and looked around. I didn't realize it then, but this was a very beautiful patch of woodland. This knowledge came only later, in retrospect and reverie, and after I had looked up the names of the trees and shrubs. There seemed to be at least one of everything, as though some-one had planted an informal paradisiacal arboretum here for the pleasure and fulfillment of the Barnes family. Here were scraggy oaks (none very tall), pines (long-leaf, short-leaf, loblolly), hickory, ash, maple, beech, juniper, sycamore, elm, cedar, walnut, pecan. As for shrubs, mesquite, of course, and those I knew because we had them in our backyard – privet, hawthorn, holly.

But to me, just then, all this was just a bewildering mix of anonymous greenery, more like an encircling army. It would have made sense to stop right there and holler for help. Dad might have heard us. But I decided, not yet. "I think he went down to the river," I told Peedo. So which way to the river? It ought to be generally downhill. "This way."

Sure enough, another hundred yards, and we could hear it. *This* Colorado, unlike the Colorado that made the Grand Canyon, was rarely dramatic or noisy. It flowed musically. In our area it was never over six feet deep, and even during spring floods there were stretches where an adult could cross the river on dry feet by judicious Olympic leaps from one sandbar to another.

We got down to the riverbank, worked our way through a maze of cypress roots, and looked around. No sign of Dad. Just the river, flowing quietly.

Peedo pointed. In a quiet eddy, just off shore, something was moving. My eyes bugged. It was the head of a snake, drifting slowly through the water, not making a ripple. I had seen snakes before. This was a big one. And he was headed straight for us. I was paralyzed. It was like in a nightmare, where you can't move and the monster comes closer and closer. He's in no hurry. He knows he has you.

Peedo laughed. "Nake!" He jumped up and down.

There was a blur of motion in the little pond. I played it back in my mind several times before I was able to figure it out. Peedo had frightened a frog hiding in the fern growth. It had jumped – in absolutely the wrong direction, straight into the gaping white maw of the snake. White – that's why they call them cottonmouths. This was a water moccasin – quite the equal of the Texas diamondback rattler in the deadliness of its venom and general irascibility. Brer Cottonmouth had probably been after that poor little frog all along. However, I had no desire to tarry for further details.

I grabbed Peedo by the arm. Terror instructed me as to our return route. We fought through the shrubs and brambles and were soon at the hilltop. Here we stopped and gasped and panted. At least now I knew where we were. Through the trees I could see (and faintly hear) the vanes of our windmill.

"Ki," said Peedo, pointing.

He was trying to say "kitty." Our cat? Out here? I looked.

It was indeed *a* cat. It was mostly hidden behind the lower branches of a cedar, but I could make out eyes, big eyes, and a big snarling mouth with lots of horrid white teeth. It was a panther.

Stiff with fear, I listened to the low scraping guttural.

I understood now why the snake hadn't harmed us. God had saved us to be eaten by this furry fiend. Today, when I think of those yellow eyes, and this scene, I think of Coleridge, and lines from "Kubla Khan".

But oh! that deep romantic chasm which slanted
Down the green hill athwart a cedarn cover!
A savage place: as holy and enchanted
As e'er beneath a waning moon was haunted
By woman wailing for her demon-lover!

At that moment, though, I didn't know about "Kubla Khan". I was having a sudden vision of Dad standing on the front porch at night, listening. Off toward the river you could hear a woman screaming. Except it wasn't a woman. "Painter," my Dad had muttered. "Painter" was what a lot of the old-timers called panthers. I knew what panthers looked like; I had seen pictures.

I wanted to grab Peedo and run, but I knew instinctively that would be fatal.

So I stood very still, my eyes darting everywhere (maybe Dad would show up), and we waited. And that's how I noted the thing in the little clearing near the big cat. It was a pile of excrement. It was bloody. Even in the dark shade of the trees it seemed to shine. And there were several tufts of cotton on the pile. Dad's cotton. The wild thought struck me that this animal had killed and eaten Dad, and that this was all that was left. And while I was thinking this, and wondering how I could break the news to Mother, the cat vanished. One moment it had been there; the next, it wasn't.

Whereupon I grabbed Peedo and we made a mad dash for the Barnes windmill.

Eventually, and piece by piece, with much eavesdropping on Mother and Dad, I put it all together. He had colon cancer. His stools were bloody. To conceal this, he moved his bowels in secret, in the woods, and wiped himself with cotton. The smell of blood had attracted the cougar.

When Dad finally got his operation, it was too late. Dad's death brought a lot of things to an end, including the religious wars. He was an agnostic. Mother was a profound Christian believer, a member of the Church of the Disciples of Christ. The denomination had been founded by Alexander Campbell in 1832, in what is now West Virginia, Mother's efforts to get Dad to join the church were fruitless. "Actually," Dad once cheerfully explained, "it's quite hopeless." According to him, old Michael Barnes (his great-grandfather) was born in Moorefield, West Virginia and was well known to Alexander Campbell. The great divine had once declared that Hell gaped for Father Barnes and all his descendants, and that there was no hope for any of us. "You see," Dad explained, "it's all set. Nothing anybody can do. So we might as well relax . . . enjoy life . . ."

But she never gave up. "Faith," she insisted. "That's all you need."

"Faith," he explained pontifically, "is believing in things that ain't so."

She prayed for him, kneeling at their bed every night. He listened with varying reactions. After a particularly knifetwisting session he'd compare her to the prayerful Mrs. Barsad, in Dickens's *A Tale of Two Cities,* always "floppin' agin' me," according to the irreverent Mr. Barsad.

"Prayer can help," Mother insisted.

"Quite true," he agreed. "For prayer reconciles you to not getting what you prayed for."

But she always won. She *knew* she was right, whereas the entire premise of his agnosticism was, he *didn't* know. He argued in quicksand.

Sometimes he would retreat in defeat up the ladder to the water tank and sit on the edge of the platform, thinking and brooding, trying to figure it all out while pretending to read the cotton news in the *Colorado Record.* He was a cotton buyer, and while he lived he made a good living as a broker.

Dad had met Mother through her voice.

The telephone company and Progress had come to Colorado City. The initial nucleus of a dozen subscribers (bank, doctor, dentist, sheriff, hotel, saloon, several cotton brokers) soon expanded exponentially to a couple of hundred. A lady was hired to help the young man operate the switchboard.

Dad had one of the new phones installed in his little office in the bank building. It was fastened to the wall and he had to stand to use it. He took the receiver down, cranked the little magneto handle on the right, and in the receiver he heard, "Number please?"

Sometimes it was a young male voice, sometimes it was a female. Sometimes he made calls just to catch her voice – sweet, lilting, rhythmic, beautifully modulated, as though she were reading from the Bible.

He sneaked into the phone office for a look.

She sat primly erect in her high-backed chair, talking softly into the apparatus hung about her neck. She wore a long thin white dress with little lace flowers covering her throat. She handled the connecting cables with deft assurance.

Dad remembers removing his hat and staring.

The office manager led him away.

The wedding was held in the Christian Church, with quite a write-up in the *Colorado Record:*

(From her Memory Book)
"Next came the Bride, erect, graceful and lovely, wearing a gown of white silk mull, silk net of yoke appliqued in ribbon embroidery, with girdle of white satin. She carried a shower bouquet of bride's roses. Her only ornament was

a diamond brooch, the gift of the groom. A cluster of orange blossoms caught from the sweet fair face the wedding veil of silk tulle, which completely enveloped her slender figure."

Perhaps we lost something when we moved to the city.

The picture taken in Fort West after the honeymoon shows him sitting, very dignified in his Sunday suit. She stands at his side, also very dignified in her long white frock with lace up to her chin, her left hand resting lightly on his shoulder. He looks very serious, almost bemused. Her expression is hard to figure out. She's smiling, but it's a Mona Lisa smile, open to the viewer's interpretation.

An unkind generic joke goes with these photographs: "He's too tired to stand up, she's too sore to sit down." I never gave much thought to my parents' sex life. None of my business. On the other hand, I thought maybe I understood her smile: she hadn't told him yet that she was pregnant with me. Probably all the women on both sides of the family knew it already, and none of the men, this being the proper nature of things.

Sometimes he would talk about "the early days." "There were no roads out here, just a few wagon ruts. It was wild. When I was a boy we still had small herds of pronghorn antelopes. They were fast – wolves and painters couldn't catch them, but you could shoot them from a buckboard with a Winchester." His face would glow momentarily, then he would sigh, and it would pass.

And then cancer, and death in a hospital in Dallas, with Mother holding his hand. Did he convert at the last minute? Or did he, like Voltaire, drive the priest from his deathbed?

Mother never talked about it.

What did we live on after he died? He left a little money – not much. And a little insurance. Again, not much. And he left an oddity – shares in a wildcat oil well currently being dug in an adjoining county by a group of optimistic Colorado City businessmen. This hole was being sunk deep into the Permian Basin, named after a famous similar geologic formation in Perm Province, Russia. The point was, lots and lots of dinosaurs, all shapes and sizes, had frolicked around in the Basin, then turned up their scaley toes and had decomposed into high-grade petroleum, all for the benefit of John D. Rockefeller and the American motorist. This particular hole hadn't hit oil yet, but "sign" kept turning up in the drill cuttings, and the locals *knew* the bit must soon strike oil.

Some predicted a gusher. So, despite no oil yet, Dad's shares had a substantial market value.

Agents of the standards (the big oil companies, that is) drove out across the bridge to Riverside and talked to Mother. They made offers. "It may never produce a drop," they warned. "Your shares could turn out to be worthless paper." All very true, she agreed. She would discuss the situation with God and let them know. Three days later she sold the shares to Sinclair Oil and deposited the certified check in the Colorado National Bank. The very next week, on a Wednesday morning, following a nitro shot, there was indeed a gusher. There was a fine picture of it in the *Record,* plus a detailed write-up.

When the nitro blew, the ground shook, and then they heard this sort of squeal – something coming up the hole, fast. And then up the derrick, and spraying out way over the top. It was a gusher, all right. But it wasn't oil. It was salt brine. And it gushed all day and all night, and all the next day, while the wind blew to all quarters, spraying salt over cotton fields for miles around. Local lawyers made a mint suing Sinclair. For days kids were bringing salt-crusted cotton bolls to school for show-and-tell.

Well, every once in a while you'll find a lake of oil under a salt dome. Let's hope Sinclair kept looking.

So Mother took her "oil" money and moved to Fort West, where she would be close to relatives and churches and schools and colleges.

Anyhow, it's easy to understand why I thought maybe there was a panther in that cave in Sycamore Creek.

And I remember that day in 1925 for another reason: on that day I knew I would become a chemist.

The Porter Chemical Co. had an ad in *The American Boy,* send away for your introductory chemical kit, twenty-five cents. Which I did. When I returned home from Sycamore Creek it was there, waiting for me, a little corrugated box of packets and vials and an instruction book. In the packets were harmless things like dyes, soda bicarb, litmus, and so on.

I put on a magic show for Mother and Peedo that very evening. The main event was to change water into wine, and back again. You put a few drops of phenolphthalein in an empty glass, then you pour in a glass of dilute soda bicarb, and the water of course turns red, because phenolphthalein is a fine pH indicator, red for bases, clear for acids. So then you add a few cc of vinegar, and the water is clear again.

Mother was dutifully amazed. Peedo (he was 7) sneered. "That's not magic. It's just a trick!"

He was probably Andersen's model for the skeptical kid in "The Emperor's New Clothes." No matter. Chemistry would overcome all criticism, all obstacles.

Champ II

One day in midterm a thing happened in chemistry class that told me she and I were bound together by a steel cable.

"This week," she began, "we will study compounds of the alkaline earth metals – magnesium, calcium, strontium, and barium. We will emphasize calcium because it's the most widely distributed of the group, and probably the most useful to us.

"It's a marvelous construction material. Our bones – and the bones of all vertebrates – are made of calcium phosphate. Without calcium, we'd look like jellyfish.

"Of the compounds, the carbonate is the commonest. For example, the foundation blocks of this building are limestone – calcium carbonate. But other calcium compounds are quite important, too. The bricks in these walls are held together with mortar made with lime – calcium hydroxide. The walls and ceiling of this very room are plaster board – calcium sulfate.

"Now there are thick limestone beds all over East Texas. And these beds have been moved up and down, under water, above water, several times during the last few million years. The water has leached out caves and holes in the stone strata. And now we come to an interesting phenomenon. What happens when water seeps through the ceiling of these limestone caves and drops to the cave floor? We assume it's saturated with calcium carbonate. So why can't the carbonate immediately precipitate?"

Her hypnotic green eyes swept the tiers. Nobody answered. We waited. "It can't," she said, "because the water is slightly acidic. And that means the carbonate isn't there as insoluble carbonate, $-CO_3$, but as soluble *bi*carbonate, $-HCO$. So now what happens? Our little water drop hangs there on the ceiling a moment, just looking around, and wondering what do do next, and while it's thinking, it's evaporating – losing solvent water. And that means it isn't saturated with bicarbonate any more. Something has to give. And the thing that happens is, two bicarbonate radicals combine, lose H_2O and CO_2, and leave one $-CO_3$ radical, which promptly finds a calcium ion and together they make calcium carbonate – which precipitates, and deposits itself either on the ceiling to form a stalactite, or on the floor, to form a stalagmite." She smiled in triumph.

"Don't you see? If this goes on for a couple of million years, the stalactite and stalagmite finally merge, and you get a beautiful limestone pillar." She walked back to her desk.

"Let's take another example. Also about calcium carbonate. From the beginning the carbonate has been the staff of life. Consider the brachiopod – a shellfish, first found in the Cambrian, some 400 million years ago. He was actually a bivalve, and looked rather like a clam. This is one of his two shells."

She held up a white circular shell three or four inches in diameter.

I went into shock. It looked exactly like Champ. *Was* it? How had *she* got it?

I realized my mouth was standing open. I closed it with a snap and continued to watch and listen intently.

She went on. "In his day he headed the evolutionary chain. He had a complex digestive system, kidneys, a nervous system, reproductive organs, muscles, and so on. This particular specimen is smooth, but many of his relatives were ribbed.

"During his formative weeks he covered his shell with a nitrogenous layer to keep it from redissolving into seawater. Under that layer he formed aragonite, a hard dense form of calcium carbonate, which would soon serve to protect him from the sea and from creatures that might want to eat him. But even aragonite eventually dissolves. So what preserved his shell after he died? How did this little piece of calcium carbonate survive for 400 million years?

"We think we know. Early on, the shell got buried in the protective mud of seas that covered this part of Texas for millions of years. Finally of course the mud changed to marl and shale, and the seas subsided and the land rose, and the marl and shale that surrounded him were broken up and washed away, leaving Brachie on the beach and forcing him to face a hostile environment. But as you can see, he was tough, and he made it through the millennia okay. And you'll find lots of others just like him, weathering out of paleozoic rocks in local river beds."

She held him up again. "You can tell he's had a hard life. One side is abraded nearly flat, and his edges are worn. That's from being tumbled around in rivers and streams. Actually, he's probably been in and out of several water courses over the past few million years, and may see several million more after we are gone."

The bell rang.

Instead of dashing for the door I hurried to her desk. "Could I see it? The shell?"

She raised her eyebrows, but handed it over. "Of course."

My hand had grown, and the shell no longer fit exactly. But it still had that tell-tale J mark. It was Champ. Slowly, I handed it back. "Thank you."

She studied me for a moment, as though going over something in her mind. Her eyes seemed to narrow, and when she next spoke her voice held a forced casualness. "I picked it up in a cave near a creek in Sycamore Park. Ever been there?"

"Sycamore . . . cave . . . ?" I repeated stupidly.

"Thousands of shells there," she said, watching me. "Along the shore . . ."

My nose twitched. It was her perfume. Delicately floral, subtle, seductive. I hadn't noticed it before. Almost as though she had just now turned it on.

She had been the creature in the cave.

"I have to go," I gasped.

I knew her eyes followed me as I scurried out the door.

In the days that followed her demeanor toward me seemed to change in subtle ways. Hard to describe. Not a teacher's pet situation. More like a heightened awareness of my existence. A watchfulness. I wasn't sure I liked it. Not that she took any special notice of me. She didn't look my way any oftener than toward the other kids. Quite the contrary, sometimes it seemed she was deliberately avoiding looking at me. Which in a way was worse than staring.

It stayed that way until the end of the semester. In June I graduated, and of course it stopped. But it left a ringing in my mind, as though it was still going on, like a tune that haunts you.

Lukey

She lectured on phosphorus one day. "Absolutely vital to life. Our teeth and bones are made of calcium phosphate. As adenosine triphosphate it supplies energy to the three trillion cells of our bodies. It's an essential plant nutrient, which the farmer furnishes as phosphate fertilizer. In nature it occurs as phosphate rock, which is totally insoluble, and which we treat with sulfuric acid to give soluble superphosphate fertilizer."

She held up two jars. "Both contain sticks of elemental phosphorus, both under water. This one is red phosphorus. It's relatively harmless." She put it down. "But *this* one – *white* phosphorus – is dangerous. It looks like a harmless white candle. It isn't." She unscrewed the lid, lifted the stick out with tongs. "It glows in the dark – that's where it gets its name. You can't see the glow just now, of course, too much light. In the dark, if I streak it along a surface, it will leave a phosphorescent mark. And I'm warning you now, don't try it. Exposing it to any kind of friction tends to ignite it. Then it spatters. Burning pieces bore into your skin and may start cancerous lesions. White phosphorus is deadly. It was used in incendiary bombs during the war. Thomas Edison learned the dangers too late. He burnt down a freight car with white phosphorus."

This was of particular interest to several of us, because our extracurricular science club actually possessed a stick of white phosphorus, at present safely preserved in a jar of water.

From the corner of my eye I noted a thoughtful expression on the face of Lukey Gruen.

This was not good.

Lukey was a charter member of our club. He had bought most of our chemicals with his rather affluent allowance and consequently had special privileges. And he had prestige: he had the distinction of longest endurance in his closed garage while burning sulfur, and we had great respect for him. But in this thing he was wrong.

The club discussed it that evening. "It's Mother's turn to host the TOGs," he said. The TOGs were a local church group. TOG stood for Truth of God, which is to say, the Bible versus Science. They had a logo, consisting of scales with the Bible in one pan and Satan holding *The Descent of Man* in the other pan. The Bible far outweighed Satan and the book.

He gave us the whole story.

His mother craved the vote for the year's most spectacular exhibit for hosting the TOGs.

The competition was fierce. Already Mrs. Crowder had pulled off a ten-minute skit of the Prodigal Son, complete with authentic ragged costumes. Hardly had the excitement subsided over that when Mrs. Beauford presented her miracle of the coin – a silver dollar in the mouth of a fish – in this case a big whiskery catfish from the bottom of the Trinity. And then there was talk about Nadine Jones's preparations for *next* month. Her husband was a chemist at the Fort West water works, and it was rumored he would (Prohibition notwithstanding) help her put on the Marriage at Cana, and change water into wine.

Mrs. Gruen perceived that desperate measures were called for. Her son was taking this esoteric incomprehensible course at JimBowie called chemistry. She bribed, she cajoled, she threatened. *Think,* Lukey! What can we come up with?

Here's what he came up with: he would draw the logo on the living room wall with a phosphorus stick, then turn off the lights, and the lines would glow in the dark, to the delight, amazement, and mystification of Mrs. Gruen and guests.

He got ready. He practiced with pencil and paper. He knew the outline by heart.

"Lukey," I said (again), "it's like striking a match. Any friction, it'll catch fire. A phos fire is hard to put out. Wilson was right. Don't do this."

"Don't worry, Joe, I'll be extra careful."

So Lukey took our jar of phosphorus.

The guests duly arrived, and Mrs. Gruen turned off the lights and seated them in whispering clusters on sofa and chairs opposite the demonstration wall.

We watched through the side window. Lukey was a fair artist, but he was slow, trying to get it just right. "Hurry," his mother told him, "I'd like to start serving in a few minutes." That was the wrong thing to say. He hurried. He zipped along. I could almost smell our phosphorus stick sizzling, oxidizing. He bore down as he sketched out Satan's head, complete with horns. Oh boy.

Yes, of course the magic crayon chose that instant to ignite. Lukey howled and dropped the burning brand. His mother howled pretty good, too. The guests didn't seem to know what to do. Their responses lacked uniformity. Mrs. Carter jumped up and down and screamed. Betty Bromley put her hands over her eyes and hollered "O God O God . . ." The rest seemed paralyzed.

We rushed in the side door and scooped up our precious phosphorus in a stack of napkins. We smothered it, but it was about gone. Sixty-eight cents. Lukey disappeared into the kitchen, and we heard water splashing. His mother was close behind. They came back into the room with wet towels, and with a few well-aimed stomps and slaps soon had everything under control.

The ladies subsided. Lukey and I joined them for one last look at the great, if catastrophic, mural. Nearly all the lines were now invisible. Only hints had survived. Bible, scales, and Darwin's opus were gone. The diabolical face was blurring into non-existence in stages, Cheshire-like. The horns first, then the pointed ears, leaving something looking horridly human. The right eye flickered. The imago was *winking* – straight at me. And then gone. But I knew then that I would remember that face forever. And the thing that named it: *phos-phorus* – light-bearer – Lucifer.

I thought it wise to depart, with Lukey still staring – at nothing. Just staring.

He showed up in class next day, rather subdued, and with his right hand bandaged and a strip of gauze across his forehead. He smelled of medication. "Yeah," he admitted to me, "it really spattered." Aside from that it was hard to understand why Lukey was so shook up. His mother won the TOG contest, hands down. Her Toll-House cookies and home-made peach ice cream quite overwhelmed the final trace odors of singed rug.

Miss Wilson repeated some of her phosphorus lecture but without mentioning any names. Her eyes seemed to keep coming back to me, but without really looking at me. Blaming me for Lukey's mishap? No, I didn't think so. It was something else, perhaps something involving Champ? Or maybe I was just imagining things? No, I wasn't. On that summer day in 1925 she had been in that cave. Why? And my interest in Champ had apparently proved to her that I had been the boy at the cave entrance. So what?

Another oddity: Lukey changed, in subtle but fundamental ways. He got religion. He started going to church every Sunday with his mother, with prayer meetings Wednesday nights. I got him off by himself. "Lukey, *why?*"

"It was the eyes of that phosphorus devil. Boring into me, talking to me, telling me I belonged to him. Joe, it was terrible."

Library Passes

Once in a while she would give me a library pass. But it wasn't enough. I needed more passes. So I stole a dozen blanks from her desk. (Yes, shame-ful.) I practiced forging her name until I had it down perfect. From then on, from time to time during study periods, I "crashed" the library. I devoured the science books first: chemistry, physics, astronomy, zoology. Slosson's *Creative Chemistry,* de Kruif's *Microbe Hunters*. Nothing on evo-lution, of course. Next, the great novelists, Hugo, Conrad, Austen, Dostoevsky, Tolstoy. I became a super-speed reader.

One afternoon late in the term as I turned in my forged slip to the attractive gray-haired librarian, Miss Meigs, she said rather noncommit-tally, "Joseph, can you wait here a moment."

Now, believe it or not, at that time there was a side of me that wished I would be caught and punished for my deceit. I had always assumed that these glorious days of reading freedom couldn't last, that I'd eventually be discovered. So here it was. I sighed and braced myself. We waited until the kids behind me handed in their passes and disappeared into the stacks and tables.

Miss Meigs was a small, spare woman, cheerful and helpful, but with a strong jaw and fire in her eye. She walked with quick grace as she monitored her little kingdom, which she ruled with iron whispers. She wore beautiful clothes, said to be bought at Neiman-Marcus in Dallas, exquisite muted pastels in summer, stunning darker woolens in winter. There were hints that she had extra income, above and beyond her meager librarian's salary. Was there a tasty secret here? A rich gentleman friend? She deflected all questions with a disarming smile.

Miss Meigs said to me, "You seem to be in here quite a bit."

I swallowed nervously.

"Pretty often, I guess."

She studied me carefully.

"You read a lot?"

"Yes, ma'am, I guess so."

"Miss Wilson says you can type sixty words a minute."

I gulped. This conversation was taking an odd turn. How would Cybele Wilson know (or *care*) how fast I typed? "Yes, I guess so."

"Spell 'all right.'"

I knew what she wanted.

"Two words."

She thought a moment. "'Agincourt.'"

I blinked. I knew what it was: the great victory of Henry's archers over the French knights, but I had never heard it pronounced before. I spelled it, and she smiled.

Miss Meigs, it turned out, was writing a book about the Hundred Years' War. She needed a lot of typing done, and we made a deal. I would work for her after school, on an Underwood in the library reference room, at 10¢ a page. It was good money. At home we could eat a little better. Maybe I would start buying lunch at school: a big five-cent two-part Mars Honey Almond candy bar.

Later that afternoon we had an interesting introductory session.

She looked at me very seriously. "Joseph, let's keep the project secret."

"Yeah, sure."

"Now, when you get to page 188, stop there, skip over to page 202, and resume typing from there. Okay?"

"Yes, ma'am."

Well, now . . . Somehow this reminded me of Miss Brown's reading assignments for Scott's *Lady of the Lake*, back at Dyess Junior High. "Skip lines so and so, pick up again at line so and so." What was it she didn't want us to read? So we all read the skipped lines very carefully. It jumped right out – all about "the ruined maiden." Okay it took only a few minutes speed-reading to discover what Miss Meigs hadn't wanted me to type. It was a sizzling bedroom episode between Henry and Catherine of Valois, which somehow even Shakespeare had missed. But this was only part of the need for secrecy. If it ever got out that Miss Meigs was writing a book, the fact would mark her as *different*. Questions would be asked. What is in this book? (Actually, gore and sex!) Is it suitable for our teenagers? Has she written other books? Yes, she had – and under a *pseudonym*! Oh dear!

Ah, Miss Meigs, you have hidden depths!

And Cybele Wilson had set it all up.

Why?

The Ford Coil

After class one day I followed Miss Wilson back into the lab bay. She turned, and I got it out, all in one sentence. "I'd like to try an experiment."

"Oh?"

I was never really comfortable when I was near her. My crotch itched, and I fought a tendency to stammer. I went on hurriedly. "I've read up on it. I know it will work. It's a process for fixing nitrogen. We run air past a spark. The nitrogen and oxygen react, and we get nitrogen oxides, probably a mix, nitrous, nitric, and so on. We bubble that into water and test for acid."

Her white lab coat wasn't buttoned. It hung loose about her. I didn't dare look, but I knew what lay behind the coat. I sensed legs, undergarments, armpits. I could reach out and touch her breasts. I closed my eyes briefly and prayed for self-control. My prayer was heard. The lab coat swirled shut, closing the doors, as it were, but simultaneously releasing an invisible cloud of perfume. I had a sudden impossible impression that the gesture was deliberate, that she had fully intended to flood me with that scented signature.

She wore no makeup, and needed none. Her cheeks were smooth and pink, her lips full and rich and just inches away. I could bend my neck and kiss this mouth that held no lipstick. Careful, Joe!

She looked at me curiously. "The Norwegians did that."

"Not exactly. They used a hot carbon arc. They have lots of cheap electricity, from water power."

She smiled at me. And there was that strange perfume again, a suggestion of flowers. "We'd need a very hot spark." I didn't catch the pronoun right away. It took a moment.

"We'd use a Ford coil, 16,000 volts minimum."

And so we set it up – she and I, and a week later we tried it out, and it worked beautifully. She let me use her personal pH meter. In an hour we got the collection liquid down to pH 3.5, and you could actually taste the very dilute nitrous/nitric acid. By then I had identified her scent: bluebonnets. Good choice. Texas's state flower.

We showed it off to the principal, Mr. Vachel, who hadn't the faintest idea what was going on, and to Mr. James, the physics teacher, who said, "So *that's* it!" What he meant was, our sparks were broadcasting static into crystal radio sets in his nearby classroom, where he was trying to teach the elements of radio. So we checked with him before scheduling future demonstrations.

So much for nitrogen fixation.

That Ford coil itself is quite another story. Here's how I happened to have it.

Three years before, on a pleasant May afternoon in study hall at Bagley Junior High (I was fourteen) I was reading an issue of *Amazing Stories.* This was the "annual," a big thick thing with a novel-length story by Edgar Rice Burroughs having to do with the adventures of John Carter on Mars, and mostly how he got his mate, the beautiful Princess Dejah Thoris, out of various terrible scrapes.

A hairy hand descended. The hand grasped the top of the magazine and extracted it from my startled fingers.

I looked up. It was the hand of the principal, Mr. Dyess. "Any more?" he hissed. He hissed in order not to distract adjacent pupils from their legitimate studies. It did not have that effect. He had a hiss like Kipling's cobra. On an earlier occasion when Lukey Gruen had been caught reading that wonderful magazine *Ballyhoo,* Mr. Dyess had hissed and the janitor had rushed in thinking that a steam pipe had broken.

I shrank into my seat. Slowly, sadly, I pulled out three more from my oversized looseleaf notebook. Collectively they contained E.E. Smith's "Skylark of Space", David Keller M.D.'s "Revolt of the Pedestrians", H.G. Wells's story about a miller who was eaten (mill and all) by a subterranean monster. And all with those wonderful detailed illustrations by Frank Paul. Oh God!

"Come with me," said the cobra.

I slunk out behind him in red-faced humiliation. I knew what was next. A locker check. Yes, he got two *Thrilling Wonder Stories*. Nobody had told me I couldn't. Nobody had warned me I risked confiscation, maybe even expulsion. It was the incomprehensible adult world at work again. What's good? What's bad? No way to know until it's all over. For a moment I thought I might remind him that the famous Mendeleev loved science fiction and in fact died while reading Jules Verne's *Journey to the Center of the Earth*. But on second thought I decided he had probably never heard of the great Russian inventor of the periodic table, and I'd be in even deeper trouble. I kept my mouth shut.

My treasures went their mournful way to the city dump, along with exudate from the cafeteria and dregs of twenty schoolroom wastebaskets.

Okay, B. Walter Dyess. You win this round, I thought. I can handle it. Anyhow, I'll soon be leaving your silly little school forever, because in the fall I'll be going on to JimBowie High. But I'll be thinking about you.

Which brings me to the Ford coil.

In 1927–28 Henry Ford stopped making Model T Fords and brought out his wonderful new Model A, completely redesigned and modernized. The Model A had a brand new ignition system. It didn't use the old Ford ignition coil. And as the old Model Ts slowly collapsed and were taken away to junk yards, a lot of the old coils were tossed into trash cans in auto repair shops.

What was this Ford coil, once the soul of the little automobile, but now cast aside as worthless? What it was, was a very efficient induction coil, which is to say, the core was a bundle of bare iron wires, wrapped in several layers of insulated copper wire, and this assembly (the primary circuit) was positioned within the secondary circuit – a very thick coil of thousands of turns of very fine insulated copper wire. In use in the car, a standard six-volt battery fed current into the primary circuit, whereupon the bundle of magnet wires pulled down a key on the top of the box. That broke the circuit, and the failing circuit in the primary was duly induced into the secondary coils, with attendant voltage amplification. With no circuit in the primary, the key was no longer attracted to the magnet core, and it sprang back up, thereby once again closing the circuit, and then the process was repeated. The intermittent current generated in the secondary circuit produced a strong spark in sequence in the four spark plugs of Mr. Ford's Model T. Six volts was boosted to 16,000. It was the ultimate induction system.

After the passage of a full year in JimBowie High School one might think that I had forgotten Mr. Dyess and what he had done to me. No. It still ached and rankled. I waited, and plotted, and schemed. Finally it all started coming together.

I knew that Mr. Dyess had very recently turned in his old Model T for a brand new Model A, which was now the envy of the neighborhood. For my revenge I needed a Ford coil. I went down to the Ford agency on Commerce, and they gave me Mr. Dyess's old Ford coil for free, gratis. How to power the coil? Once more I lucked out.

Mr. Dyess's splurge into modern marvels had not stopped with Mr. Ford's new car. I knew that he had bought a new, powerful ten-tube RCA radio that required no batteries. You simply plugged it into the wall. I kept an eye on his garbage. Sure enough, he threw out his old five-tube radio and its attendant cluster of batteries: two forty-five–volt Bs, a six-volt A, and a four-and-a-half–volt C. A veritable treasure. I swooped as soon as the drop was made.

Actually, all I proposed using were the two Bs, for ninety volts. I figured if six volts from an auto battery would convert to 16,000, ninety volts would convert to fifteen times 16,000, for a total of a quarter million volts. I suspected that Marconi had spanned the Atlantic with less in 1901.

As a preliminary test I hooked up the Ford coil to our hundred-twenty–volt house current. I put the rheostat on low and grabbed the electrodes. Just a tingle. I turned up the rheo. More tingle. I frowned, turned it up to ninety volts and grabbed the electrodes once more. I felt a numbing convulsion, then a momentary blackout. I regained consciousness on the other side of the room.

My little brother Peedo was standing in the doorway, pointing at me, and howling with laughter. I looked up at the bureau mirror, and I could see why. My hair was standing out straight – like the quills of a porcupine. Whereupon I lost all dignity. It broke me up too.

I had blown a fuse, of course. Wonder I wasn't killed. If I had gone the full one-twenty, maybe I would have been. But okay, it worked fine at ninety, and that's all I needed to know.

As my broadcasting antenna I would use Mrs. Dyess's backyard galvanized wire clothesline. For a ground I used Mr. Dyess's backyard hydrant. I set it up in the shelter of his peach trees. If perchance he looked out his kitchen window, he would see nothing amiss. He would not see that his own possessions were treacherously turning on him, nor that he was being hoisted on his own petard, nor by whom. He would miss the irony, but that was okay.

To monitor the event I had brought along my own little crystal set, which consisted of one thousand turns of enameled wire coiled around a cylindrical Quaker Oats box, a little condenser, and a galena crystal complete with tickler. I didn't have earphones – just a telephone receiver "found" in a vacant house. We passed it around within our club according to need, like the three Norns rotating Wotan's eyeball. I had scheduled the day and the hour carefully. For this Saturday afternoon it was mine.

All was ready. I held the telephone receiver to my ear and listened a moment. I heard cowbells, then the announcer:

"Good afternoon, folks. Yes, you are listening to Radio Station WBAP, the voice of Fort West, and this afternoon we will be bringing you the crucial game of the Southwest Conference, Southern Christian versus Southern Methodist, with kickoff time in one minute exactly. The Frogs won the toss and will receive –"

I touched the transmitter key. And jerked. The buzz in my telephone receiver was deafening. For a moment I was afraid Mr. Dyess heard it all the way from his parlor. But no. He had other concerns. He hadn't heard my little buzz. He couldn't have. It was totally submerged under the raucous rumble of my brief transmission as received by his super extraordinary magnificent brand-new RCA, with the new superheterodyne circuit and floor-shaking volume – the machine that (he hoped) would carry him to fame and fortune.

For Mr. Dyess was entertaining three members of the Dallas County School Board, and it was rumored that they were considering him for Superintendent of Schools for Dallas County. Now, Fort West and Dallas were bitter rivals in just about everything. He had invited them in to listen to the game as Dallas fans. I considered him to be an out-and-out traitor. I pictured him now, frowning, wondering where that awful static had come from. And then smiling and turning back to his guests. Just momentary, fellows. Nothing wrong with the radio. See, the game is still on.

With my transmission key in my hand I relaxed and lay back comfortably under his peach trees.

From time to time, as SMU got the ball, Mr. Dyess's radio was drowned in static. Not once did I let his radio announce a winning play or a score for Dallas. And this went on, and on . . .

Until . . .

I looked up. My jaw dropped. It was Helen Dyess, the Enemy's only daughter. She was a year behind me in school, and a year younger. But she had already begun to fill out. She wore one of those tasteless straight-up-and-down dresses, but it didn't hide the fact that she was very pretty.

Her dark brown hair was fluffed out in curls around her head, in imitation (I supposed) of a favorite movie star (Norma Shearer?). She wore flat-heel shoes and white socks that reached to just above her ankles. Her chin was lifted slightly, not in arrogance, but in the secret confidence of a girl who knows she is rapidly becoming a woman.

I sighed and got to my feet. Her brown eyes went from me to the equipment, and back to me. She put her hands on her hips. "I know what you're doing."

And I knew I was in trouble, and not merely with His Satanic Majesty. What I was doing was against the law, of course. Radio jamming is okay only if done on a big scale by governments.

I didn't know what to say. I just kept looking at her, and thinking, gosh, I wish we could like each other. Eventually I stammered, "How did you know I was here?"

"My braces tingled – and *tasted.* I just followed the taste."

"Oh." I had to think about that.

"He's got some people in there from Dallas." Her expression was hard to decipher.

"Yeah, I'd heard that."

"They might want him to move to Dallas."

I got it. She didn't want to move. She didn't know any kids in Dallas. All her friends were here in Fort West. I said, "So what do you think? Are they going to hire him?"

"I don't know. Every time he got static, they looked at each other – kind of funny."

"Sixty seconds left in the game," I said. "SMU is getting ready to kick a field goal – twenty-five yards – for a tie." I offered her the transmission key.

She shook her head. "Joe, I can't. He's my father."

"Yeah."

"*You* do it."

"But –"

"You do it, or I'll tell," she said. "Please," she added.

So all this effort, all this exquisitely plotted vengeance, was indeed going to sabotage his career, but for all the wrong reasons. What kind of revenge is *that?*

I glared at Helen Dyess and I pressed the key and held it down.

We listened to the muted buzzing from the house. After a long time I stopped, and it stopped.

Soon after, we heard cars starting up. You could tell they were important people: their cars had the new automatic starters. You didn't have to crank and risk a broken arm. His guests weren't wasting any time leaving.

Helen stood close. "Thank you, Joe. You may kiss me." She waited. I was paralyzed. "Are you afraid?" She laughed. "Wow, how you blush. Really, Joe . . ." She pulled my head down and hugged me and kissed me hard on the lips. I felt the pressure of her body, all up and down mine, her tummy, her hard little breasts. I was going to put my arms around her, but she stepped away It was just as well – I was getting an erection. Which she damn well knew – the little minx. As she turned away into the peach trees she called back, "Juliet was thirteen . . . same as me."

I rubbed my mouth and looked after her.

Mongolia Paper Co.

Various things were happening in 1933, big things . . . little things . . . in- between things, depending on where you sat. Hitler was appointed German chancellor. Franklin Roosevelt was inaugurated as president. James Hilton's *Lost Horizon* had a long waiting list at the Public Library. Including me, but they never got to me. Lines formed around the block to see *King Kong* at the Palace. Irrelevant. I had no money to see it.

Anyhow, I had other concerns.

In 1933 I graduated from high school, turned my paper route over to Peedo, and started looking for a real job. I answered ads. I trod all streets.

I knew shorthand, I knew typing. But when they wanted a stenographer, they hired a girl. That was the custom.

Did I have any marketable qualifications that a lady stenographer didn't have? I figured there must be something, somewhere. I kept looking.

From seeing Cybele Wilson five times a week, with graduation the frequency had precipitously dropped to zero. The deprivation was doing odd things to me. Sometimes when I thought about her I had the sensation of falling into an infinitely deep black hole, and I'd have trouble getting a full breath.

I knew she lived in an apartment in Edwards Court, a little street that dead-ended in a scattering of oaks and maples and had seen better days. She parked her coupe in a graveled area adjoining the complex.

During the days I was looking for a job I liked to walk by Edwards, on the off chance I might see her, perhaps going to or returning from her car, or maybe just stepping out of the apartment entrance to get the morning paper. But I never did. I knew she was there. Sometimes her car was there, sometimes it was gone.

Sunday mornings she drove to St. Joseph's for the service there. This ruled out trying to catch a glimpse of her on Sundays, because I had to attend church with Mother during the same hours.

Where persistence failed, chance succeeded. I caught a glimpse of her downtown.

It was on Friday, in the last week of August, 1933. I was coming out onto the street after a futile session with the Ace Employment Agency. I was wearing suit and tie, but it was hot, and I was in the process of removing my jacket, when I saw her, about a hundred yards away, coming down the steps of the Public Library. It was too far to call to her. I started trotting down the sidewalk, bumping into people.

Just then the Edwards bus drove up to the Library corner and screeched to a halt. The bus doors opened exactly opposite her. She put a foot on the step, then unaccountably turned in my direction for just a fraction of a second, then yielded to pressure from people behind her, and vanished into the bus.

I stifled a groan, and stopped. My thoughts were clouded. Had she seen me? Impossible to tell. And even if she had, would she remember me? Why should she? She could hardly be expected to remember the dozens, maybe hundreds, of students in her classes. Well, maybe she would remember. Because of the shell . . . the nitrogen fixation project . . .

I loosened my tie, slung my jacket over my shoulder, and started the long walk home.

I had barely got in the front door when the phone rang. Mother got it. "Joe, for you. Some lady?"

For a few seconds I had trouble breathing. She had seen me. I finally got everything under control and picked up the receiver. "Hello."

"Joe? Joe Barnes?"

"Yes?" It came out as a gurgle. I was shivering.

"Cybele Wilson, Joe."

"For goodness sake! Good to talk to you! How are you?"

Stupider and stupider. I wanted to call her by her first name, but I was afraid.

"Why, I'm fine, Joe, thanks. Joe, listen, was that you I saw downtown this afternoon, near the Library?"

"That was me. You were getting on the bus."

"Yeah. Are you working this summer?"

"I'm looking. I haven't found anything."

"Joe, I know you type. Do you take shorthand?"

"Yeah."

"Look, I have heard of an opening for a male stenographer who can also do some heavy physical work."

"Ah?" My heart skipped several beats. *A real job?* Oh God!

"It's in a rough neighborhood, though. Would you be interested?" She sounded so diffident, so polite, that it sounded as though I was doing her a big favor just to think about it.

She gave me the address. Mongolia Paper Co. East Second Street. Talk to the manager, Mr. Feingarten. "They're still open. Call him now." She gave me the number. "Good luck, Joe." I stammered a goodbye.

Of course, it would have been perfectly normal if I had asked her how she had learned of this opening. I didn't. The fact of a genuine job possibility overwhelmed everything. I didn't even think about it.

I immediately phoned Mr. Feingarten. He was non-committal. He asked some questions. "Age? You type? Shorthand? Height? Weight? Come see me Tuesday." That was next week, the day after Labor Day.

"What does it pay?" I asked.

"Fourteen a week." It sounded like a challenge. Like, you want to make something of it?

No, I didn't. On the contrary. I thought, fourteen a week! A fortune! If I got the job.

East Second Street

The early Texas settlers got to name their new towns pretty much as they pleased. So there were a lot of highly descriptive names, such as Bee Cave, Cactus, Calf Creek. And the displaced Indians were remembered: Waxahachie (meaning "Cow River"), Comanche, Pawnee. Optimism (or was it sarcasm?) produced Eden, Utopia, Elysian Fields. Humor was not absent: Gun Barrel, Point Blank, Bangs. Some were melodious: Rising Star, Rolling Meadows, The Woodlands. Some were just plain inexplicable: Dime Box, Uncertain, Cut-and-Shoot. Technology was recognized: Telegraph, Telephone. Some were taciturn: Arp, Dew, Hye. If they found water, even a trickle, they praised God and put water in the town name: Sweetwater, Apple Springs, Buffalo Springs. So it's easy to understand that Fort West was never formally founded or chartered or whatever it is you do to bring a town into official existence.

In the mid–eighteen hundreds Brigadier General William Jenkins West of Mexican War fame camped briefly by the Trinity River in a sort of admonitory action against hostile Comanches. That was Camp West. The War Department improved on the idea and called it Fort West, but then moved all the soldiers out. The Indians resented the implication they were not worth fighting, and so they packed up and moved to West Texas, where they held center stage for a long time.

But back to General West.

Long after the War (between the states, that is) the city fathers proposed erecting a bronze equestrian statue to the general, in what was then West Square, just south of where the courthouse was being built. There was a lot of heated discussion and internal dissension about this. First and foremost, should a statue be erected at all, since a fair number of the burghers thought the general was a Yankee.

This was a very serious matter, and the City Council appointed a snoop committee to look into it. And sure enough, the committee found that General West had been born in Hudson, New York, March 1, 1794.

The Council held a hurried session. Alternate names were considered. Minutes of the meeting were recorded by a court reporter who used the new Pitman shorthand. Excerpts survive, thus:

"Robert E. Lee?"

"Already took."

"Stonewall Jackson?"

"Took."

"Jeff Davis?"

"Took."

"Travis?"

"Tooken."

"Houston?"

They went down the list, Austin, Crockett, Bowie, all the early Texas heroes. All already taken. Next, Confederate heroes. Other towns had already grabbed them, too.

A big Texas & Pacific Railroad executive was present at the Council session. He spoke:

"Gentlemen, in 1849, forty-two men of Company F, Second Dragoons in General West's Brigade, established a camp here. I was top sergeant in that company. We served under the general in the Mexican War. *I* named the camp for the general. I am now a director and substantial stockholder in the T & P, presently stalled thirty miles east of here, in Dallas. Our board will meet next week and decide whether to come on in here to Fort West. I like the name Fort West. I like it a lot. On the other hand, I appreciate your problem. Gentlemen, as an alternate name, consider this. A great many Texas towns have been named or renamed after railroad officials: Baird, for Matthew Baird of the T & P; Taylor, Houston Belt and Terminal; Richardson, for Texas & New Orleans. So, in this emergency, I offer my own name, again on behalf of the T & P."

"You all's full name, sir?"

"Sherman Butler Grant. But I assure you, no relation to any of *them.*"

Somebody whispered: "Just the three most hated Yankees in history."

The room was quiet.

Mayor Sanders said, "Gentlemen, I offer a resolution."

Apparently he spoke slowly and with precision, and the reporter had no difficulty getting it all down:

"Council Resolution Number One, 1873. Through sad error, and by no fault of his own, General William J. West was born in New York State. His sympathies however were always with Texas. Our fair city will continue to be named after him."

After that, there was no question about *whether* the statue of General West would be put up, just when, and also where was the money. It finally got very handsomely erected in 1907, just in time to be melted down in the big fire of 1909. Fort West had other, less contentious names. An early one was Panther City. In 1888, on the morning of the day the brand new courthouse awaited its dedication ceremony, early comers noted that a cougar was resting peaceably on the front steps. Now, you know how a plain house cat will sit in your chair by the radiator and radio, and eye you in puzzled askance when you come in and ask it to move. Well, the cougar didn't want to move. This caused excitement in the gathering audience. Of course, you can just swat a cat with a rolled-up newspaper, and it will get the message. But nobody wanted to try that with the cougar.

Mayor Sanders (yeah, they kept re-electing him) arrived in his carriage, followed by the sheriff and a couple of deputies on horseback. Next, a photographer, complete with tripod and glass plates. Everything fell into place after that. The mayor, in a burst of insanity, bravado, and with an eye on the governorship, stepped down out of his carriage (and high time, for the horses smelled the big cat and were trembling and sweating and ready to bolt). He called over to the photographer, "Get your flash ready, Zeke!"

"All set, Your Honor!"

His Honor walked up the steps and stood by the critter (who looked up at him curiously). Wearing an expression that said, "Fort West is the greatest town in the State of Texas," the mayor pointed down at the feline and hollered over to Ezekiel Billmeyer, Professional Photographic Portraits, One Dollar, Satisfaction Guaranteed, "Hit it, Zeke!"

A *bang*. A *yowl*.

When the white cloud of magnesium oxide settled, the cat was gone, together with two horsemen and a boy on a mule.

Zeke Billmeyer's picture eventually made every major paper across the continent, then crossed the seas and confirmed to readers of the London *Times* and Paris's *Le Monde* opinions they had long held regarding the state of civilization in America.

Today, in the phone book we see Panther City Oil Co., Panther City Restaurant, Panther City Morticians, and so on. The JimBowie school paper was the Pantherette, their football team was the Panthers.

Alternate names didn't stop there. Mayor Sanders never made it to the governor's mansion in Austin, but he did get three more railroads into the city, coming in from the east and north, and going out again, west and south. And that brought the cattle drives, and the stockyards on the North Side, which could be smelled all the way to Cleburne when the wind was right. So we became Cow Town.

The rails were wonderful. They stuck like tree roots into the sides of the city; actually, in places, right into the heart and throat. Some of the sidings came within two blocks of the courthouse: for example, the spur on East Second Street. The courthouse is on Weatherford Street. Next, going south, is First Street. Then Second Street. *East* Second Street is Second Street east of Main Street.

There were livery stables and shops and warehouses and little factories all up and down East Second Street, and to serve them, a rail spur. In earlier times a little yard loco would push a string of box cars up onto the spur, and then the engineer and fireman and brakeman might knock off for a few hours. They would visit houses in the district. And so that they could be found in an emergency, or collected if drunk, they left a red lantern burning in a front window of the house in question. It was probably this way in thousands of Red Light communities in thousands of American railtowns.

So – this was my first job. The Mongolia Paper Company, on East Second Street, the heart of the red light district. I was seventeen.

On that first Tuesday morning I walked down the middle of the gravel street, headed for my job interview. There were no sidewalks. It was a few minutes before eight, but some of the girls were up already. Or maybe they hadn't gone to bed yet.

They had a technique, unobtrusive, but explicit. They sat crossways in a front window, pulled back their skirts to expose a leg almost to the crotch, and they whistled. The whistle was artistic, seductive, yet artless, like a Mozart flute adagio. Most girls can't whistle. These could.

I lowered my head and passed on.

The last house was at the intersection of East Second and Sandt Streets. It was bigger than the others, with two, maybe two and a half stories, and it was catty-cornered across the street from the paper company.

A grizzled old man sat in a rocking chair on the front porch, rocking slowly and smoking a corncob pipe. I nodded to him, and he nodded back.

And so on to Mongolia's loading dock and entrance. After a brief discussion Mr. Feingarten hired me. I knew he would.

Mr. Feingarten was a small heavy man, long resigned to the claims of an immense cirrhotic liver. He had snapping black eyes, a monk-like fringe of black hair circling cautiously around a bald pate. He wore horn-rim glasses and was continually wiping white flecks from them with the tip of his necktie. Like the monsoons of India dandruff rained eternally from copious inexhaustible eyebrows. To make a point he would remove his glasses, thrust them at his audience, wipe them with his necktie, then replace them in a quick reflexive gesture. I could sense that it was all automatic, that he did not know he did this.

For the next three years I wrestled with two-hundred-pound rolls of wrapping paper, near-weightless boxes of Dixie cups, clumsy bundles of corrugated boxes. I loaded the ancient truck. I unloaded box cars. Intermittently I typed letters to people who owed money, There were forms. Dear Bill: I know you've overlooked . . . Dear George, We shall expect something on account . . . Dear Rod: If we don't hear from you by . . .

At noon everybody knocked off for lunch. It was my job to go up to the Big House and pick up the boss's sandwich (roast beef, Swiss cheese, lettuce, tomato) and Coke. Madame Diana Mulligan made it for him personally.

On Saturdays we worked half a day. At twelve noon Mr. Carey, the bookkeeper, counted out my fourteen dollars. That's 280 loaves of bread. A dizzying thought. There were not that many loaves in all the Piggly Wigglies in Fort West.

At first the work was hard. As the bundles of grocery bags and rolls of wrapping paper came in by truck or boxcar they had to be carted into the warehouse and stacked. And then, sometimes in the same day, carted out again to the delivery truck. My work clothes dripped sweat. At night, after supper (beans and toast) I collapsed into bed. If I moved, my muscles shrieked. ʾ

And then, all of a sudden, everything became easy, almost effortless. I was doing the same heavy work, but my muscles no longer ached: they had turned to concrete. I stopped sweating. (Well, maybe just a little, on a long hot day, with a lot of orders to fill.)

I saved money by routinely walking the four miles to work. The combination of leg, gut, back and arm exercises had a curious effect on my body.

Example: I needed underwear.

On the way home one day I stopped by Striplings to buy a couple of pair (fifty cents a pair). The saleslady said, "What size?" I didn't know. She got out a tape measure. I sucked in my gut. She measured twenty-two inches. She looked at me dubiously, picked out some boxer shorts. I paid. When I got home I tried on a pair. I couldn't get them on. My thighs were thicker than my waist. I had to exchange them.

So now I understood the figures of those Greek hoplites on vases from B.C. Athens, Sparta, Thebes. I knew why they had those big muscular legs and wasp-waists: they marched twenty miles a day carrying a shield, spear, and full pack. We see this clearly in the pottery of the time. Achilles slaying Penthesileia, British Museum, typical.

In this last week of May I sat in the back row at the old high school and watched the graduation ceremonies. The year before, I had received my own diploma here. I had arrived early, hoping to get a glimpse of Cybele Wilson. I got a look at everybody as they came in. No Cybele. Maybe she was late? No. There was no requirement, no tradition that she attend. She never showed. I figured I might as well leave, go home. But then I noticed that Helen Dyess was on the program. This might be worth staying for. In fact, she was valedictorian. She made a fine speech, just a teensy shaky at first, but after that she came on strong. I just watched her and admired. She was so pretty. A young woman now. Her dark hair was bobbed in the current fashion (modeled, I think, on Colleen Moore, a famous movie actress). Her black gown (rented for the occasion) hid nothing from my imagining eyes. I knew (or thought I knew) what was underneath, and the knowledge accelerated my heart beat. In the fall she would go on to Southern Christian University.

I think our eyes connected at one point, but it was across a considerable distance, with lots of people in between, and I couldn't be sure. She didn't miss a syllable.

When she was done, there was a murmur of applause, and I left.

I considered asking her for a date, but the thought soon evaporated. I didn't have any money. Every Saturday afternoon I turned my meager pay over to Mother. Anyhow I had never dated a girl before, and I'd probably mess it up. So maybe it was just as well. And how could I face Mr. Dyess? Or was it so long ago he wouldn't remember confiscating my *Amazings*?

Art Class

It rarely rained, but when it did, I didn't walk. I took the Hemphill streetcar. And on this particular rainy Saturday afternoon, so did a lot of other people. The only seat left was next to a very pretty woman. I recognized her. Mrs. Gaither, the art teacher at JimBowie. Except she had resigned from the school system and had opened her own studio. She saw me. Her eyes lit up. She smiled and motioned to me to sit by her.

We talked. That is, mostly I just answered questions. And she kept looking at me – arms, chest, legs. Was something wrong? I was wearing a short-sleeve shirt and brown denim pants. I checked my apparel covertly. Fly buttoned, at least.

She said, "Ever do any modeling?"

"Modeling?"

"Posing before an art class."

"No, never have."

"We had a young man, but he quit."

"Oh."

"You're working?"

"Yes, ma'am."

"You probably wouldn't have time?"

"Maybe not."

"And modeling isn't easy. You'd have to hold a pose for half an hour at a time. And nude, except for a – ah –

Jock strap, I thought. "Athletic support."

"Yes, that. And I can't pay much. Forty cents an hour."

I made thirty-five at Mongolia.

I knew Mother would never approve. To her the human body was an instrument of Satan and existed only for the purpose of getting you into trouble with God. It was always a mystery to me how she had managed to conceive and bear two sons.

"I have to get off at the next stop," said Mrs. Gaither. "My studio's on Travis. My Saturday class starts in half an hour. Why don't you pay us a visit? See what it's like?"

"Forty cents an hour," I murmured.

"Plus coffee and doughnuts."

I was always hungry. "Now?"

"Sure, why not?"

I reached up over her and punched the stop buzzer.

There were eight pupils in her Saturday class: five women, three men. They had already set up their easels and the women were making coffee when we arrived. She introduced me to each in turn. This was no collection of hobby-seeking dilettants. One man was an art instructor at Southwestern College. Two women worked in the layout rooms of the *Star-Telegram* and the *Press*. A man had exhibited in Houston. And so on.

They looked me over. Nothing erotic about it. I relaxed. I was just a body, an artifact, a part of the curriculum, brought here by contract for their instruction.

And Sarah Winters. She was a very attractive widow, 30-plus, brunette, pretty brown eyes. She was already an accomplished artist, and famous in her own circle. She had done the exquisite line drawings in two chapters of Cornfield's *Anatomy*. The money from this she had invested in a gold mine in Utah operated by her boyfriend, to whom she sent more money from time to time. She claimed she had a jar full of test samples from the mine. "It assays 99%, and there'll be gobs more when we get into full production."

So what was she doing here? Mrs. Gaither had promised a live male model with well-delineated musculature. She was not here to be taught anything by Mrs. G (whom she clearly disliked). She was here on a commission for a set of plates for Harvard Medical School.

Somehow, and for no immediately discernible reason, she reminded me of the beautiful and diabolical Lady de Winter in Dumas's *The Three Musketeers*.

A strange group. Despite the ever-present camaraderie there were subterranean rivalries. I quickly caught on to who hated whom and whose side each was on. They seemed to polarize around Mrs. Gaither and Sarah Winters.

Back to that first Saturday afternoon.

A few minutes after the introductions I emerged from the model's dressing closet, stripped except for jock strap. I walked to the dais, stepped up. I amazed myself. I was calm. I didn't blush. My breathing was regular. If I had any thoughts at all, they were mostly to the effect that this was very easy money, and that it couldn't last.

Mrs. Gaither came over and tapped an easel with a ruler. "Class! Today we continue our study of the musculature. And I admonish you, you cannot accurately represent the human body until you know each and every muscle and their respective skeletal attachments." She turned and studied me in brief approval. "This afternoon we continue with our study of the male torso. Mr. Barnes, will you please flex your abdominal muscles."

She tapped my gut with her ruler. "Thanks. Three of them. Big fellows. The external abdominal oblique. And this one, rectus abdominus. Number three, transverse abdominal oblique. They're a great help in just about all of our strenuous physical activities – running, jumping, throwing a spear, shooting an arrow, dancing . . ."

And so on. As the weekends fluttered by I learned a lot about the human body. I dug out the books. I studied how muscles worked, and learned about the nervous system. Of course, just posing in one position for interminable minutes could be boring, but the rest of it was fun – the strange company, the weird talk. By Christmas I had made an extra $15. For just standing there, naked. Easiest money I had ever made. I got presents for Mother, Peedo, Mrs. Gaither.

I developed a good workable tactic for avoiding boredom and muscle lock while posing. Mrs. G had hung copies of various masterpieces on the walls, showing a few men, but most of them showed women, generally in various stages of undress. I focussed on whatever female portrait I was facing during the session, and I counted the seconds required to transform her into Cybele. Sort of a self-hypnosis that permitted a long pose without flicking a muscle.

A fair copy of a Modigliani, a lady with a long face, graced the east wall. It took a real effort to change her into Cybele. Facing south was a fine copy of Rubens's *Venus at Her Toilette*. A bit overweight, but aside from that and the wrong hair color, she carried a passing resemblance to my idol. Westward was Botticelli's *Venus Rising from the Sea.* Very good. In between were copies of Manet's *Olympia* and *Luncheon on the Grass.*

I developed a grading system. How many seconds (estimated, of course) were required to change a given female figure into Cybele? For several weeks the record stood at ten seconds (Goya's *Maja Desnuda*).

Every week or so Mrs. G traded exhibits with new works brought in from storage. "They need the air," she explained. And then I might have to readjust my techniques, and my home-made rating system would change.

On one particular Saturday afternoon when I came in several of the class were clustered around a new painting, like bees buzzing around a nectar-laden flower. It was a female nude. I could see that much. A welcome sight, for it replaced a weird Picasso female who had a rating of thirty seconds.

By filtering the buzz I picked up scraps of information. Mrs. Gaither had painted the picture several years ago. The model, a friend of hers, wished to remain anonymous. That's why the face was turned away.

A woman queried, "She's holding a cup? It looks like the Cup at St. Joseph's. Is that what it's supposed to be?"

Mrs. G said, "I don't really know. She described it, and that's the way I painted it."

"The Holy Grail?" the man from Houston muttered. "Crazy."

Someone said, "At St. Joseph's, they say if you drink from the Cup, you'll totally forget your past, everything you ever did."

"That's only for just before reincarnation," someone added. "Your spirit drinks the waters of Lethe from the Cup before you enter the new body. It erases all memory of your previous life."

Mrs. G clapped her hands sternly. "Class, you'll have to finish this discussion another time. I remind you, Mr. Barnes is paid by the hour, so let's all get back to work."

They returned to their easels. From the podium, and holding a ten-pound Roman pilus that Mrs. Gaither had dug up somewhere, I finally got a good look at the new picture.

I gasped. Even though she was turned away and I could not see her face, I knew I was staring at the most gorgeous Venus portrait of my life. She was young, perhaps in her late teens. Perhaps average height, dark hair falling in burnished strands down around her shoulders. Her body, slightly turned away, showed a dimple in the left buttock. She cast no shadow on a light blue velvet backdrop. It was as though the light went right through her. And something else odd here: the cup. Where did she get it? No table to be seen. One has to look closely. She is not alone. The faint shadow of a long loose sleeve is visible on the blue backdrop. As if, in mystic ritual preceding the portrait, she has taken the cup of forgetfulness from a cowled hand.

Oh boy . . . Joe, I thought, you keep this up, you'll be just like these characters. Worse, even.

Except for the hair – wrong color, wrong length – she could have been Cybele, as so often fantasized in adoring memory, bereft of cloying clothing, standing at her lab bench, stunning in her primal beauty. I looked at this vision, and I saw Cybele immediately. I fought chills and a fever simultaneously. I knew little beads of sweat were popping out on my brow. Nobody noticed. Oh Cybele, Cybele . . .

After class I wanted to ask Mrs. G if the girl were in fact Cybele. But I was afraid. She had practically stated the model had wanted to remain unknown. It would be bad manners to come right out and ask. Maybe I could be circuitous: "Mrs. G, was she anybody I know?" No, not that either. Well, why not ask Cybele herself? Oh dear, no! Well, one day, maybe . . .

A couple of weeks later Mrs. G replaced the troublesome vision with Munch's *The Shriek,* and all was quiet once more. Mrs. Gaither announced in April that she was closing the studio in a few weeks. She was going to

Paris, to resume studies in some famous French art school. On the final Saturday, we'd have a party.

On the next-to-last Saturday Sarah Winters brought in an exhibit intended to silence all scoffers forever: something she called a gold crystal, fresh from her mine in Utah. It was wrapped in jeweler's tissue, which she unfolded carefully on the table for our awed inspection. "But don't touch!"

When I got to the head of the line I bent over and examined the little particle. It was indeed a crystal, a tiny cube; and it glittered and sparkled. Now I had read up on gold. True, this little crystal had a cubic crystalline habit. But crystals of gold were rare. According to the literature they were almost never found loose in western deposits. So what was this mysterious little sparkler? Pyrite, iron sulfide – "Fool's Gold" – was also cubic, and it also glittered.

And then I did a very stupid thing. "Sarah, your samples are supposed to assay 99%?"

"Yes, of course."

"You had them assayed?"

"My partner did. What are you driving at?" She began folding up the tissue.

"There's a simple test."

"Yeah? Like what?"

"You've got a jarful?"

"Yeah?"

"Put a pinch in a cup of acid. Do it outside. Vinegar should work. Muriatic acid is faster. You can get it from the lumber yard. Try just a sniff, no more. If you get a rotten egg smell, it's hydrogen sulfide, and it means you don't have gold. It's iron pyrite." I almost said "fool's gold." "Careful, though. H_2S can kill you. If you get that smell, throw the stuff out right away."

She listened, but she didn't answer. After a moment she simply rescued her maligned specimen and returned to her easel.

A few days before Mrs. Gaither's farewell party, Sarah phoned me at work. Would I come by after work and show her how to test her gold. Her voice sounded peculiar. Strained? Had she been crying?

I found the address. She met me at the top of the stairs and I followed her into her tiny apartment. It consisted of a combination parlor, bedroom, and kitchen, with a miniscule bathroom off to one side. I wondered if I was going to lose my virginity that evening.

I sniffed. Very faint odor of hydrogen sulfide. She had already made the test – inside. When she called me, she had known what she had. I suspected a bitter telephone call to a feckless lover in Utah, probably with screams.

"Excuse me." She went into the bathroom. After a moment the toilet flushed. She came out wearing a thin pink housecoat. The nipples of her breasts pressed against the fabric. She walked up to me and put her hand up under my loose shirt. The touch burned my gut, and I gasped. I smelled a strange tantalizing odor, musky, with a tinge of amine. I thought of Napoleon, writing Josephine from his Italian campaign: I'll be in Paris in two weeks. Meanwhile don't bathe!

She looked up at my face. And smiled. "Joe," she whispered, "abdominal oblique." Her fingers continued a restless exploration. "Rectus abdominus."

I shivered. Goosebumps raced up and down my arms and neck, like kids in a game of tag. The hands moved on. They were on my bare arms. "Biceps," she said, "to lift. Triceps – to release. Muscles come in pairs, Joe. And so do other things."

Her housecoat opened. She put my right hand on her left breast. The hand couldn't help itself. It had no will of its own. I stared down at her face. "Cybele?" It came out as a slow bewildered whisper.

"Sybyl . . . ?" She looked up at me, puzzled, her mouth open. One of her incisors was chipped.

"Sarah, I mean," I stammered. "I . . . I . . . have to go."

But she had me by the wrist. "Joe . . . no . . . stay. Here, wait." She let go long enough to refasten her housecoat, but I was gone. I didn't even say goodbye, or "see you at the party."

As I fled down the sidewalk I realized I had committed an unforgivable sin. She had assumed I had known what her invitation was all about. And then . . . this. But . . . *"Cybele?"*

I continued to walk very fast, and as I walked I thought I knew then that I would never bed a woman I did not love. I loved Cybele Wilson. I wanted her to be the first I possessed.

A fantasy. I knew that. But a fantasy so strong it had dropped a monolithic portcullis between me and a very willing and desirable female. So now, who was a little crazy?

Saturday morning, the day of Mrs. Gaither's farewell party. She called me at work from the studio. There was a terrible smell of rotten eggs in the place. "Please stop by."

I did. It was hydrogen sulfide, H_2S. In certain concentrations it can kill you. I found the source right away. It was Sarah Winters's mayonnaise jar of fool's gold, which is to say iron sulfide powder, immersed in muriatic acid. And it was bubbling away. Mrs. G looked at me, horrified. I looked back, but just shook my head.

I threw it down the toilet, cleaned everything up, we opened all the windows, and the hot May breeze soon purified the studio.

Sarah Winters was in fact probably dead by then. According to the police report in the next day's *Record-Telegram* she had accidentally left the gas on in her parlor before stretching out on the floor in her pink housecoat.

What was her point? Had she been trying to kill *me*? Mrs. G? The whole class? And why herself? It was all a ghastly mystery.

Did I feel guilty – about her death? Yes. For weeks I had nightmares about her body, lying there by the stove. It took a long time to banish the demons.

Oh, hell. I'm sorry, Sally, sorry sorry sorry –

Well, anyhow, Mrs. Gaither held the party, and after the liquor had flowed a little, we had a pretty good time. There was some frisky behavior, male and female. Mrs. G shooed them all out at eight, and I stayed behind to help sweep up.

When I left, we kissed goodbye. I never saw her again. We exchanged Christmas cards a couple of times, and then that dwindled away to nothing.

Southwest Bible College

Every morning as I walked to work the girls and I would exchange greetings. Such of them as were up and awake, anyhow. At noon, when I went up to the Big House on the corner for the boss's Coke and sandwich, I always said hello to Mr. Sandt, the old man who sat on the porch, rocking slowly away in his chair, smoking his pipe and occasionally getting up to spit over the railing into the scrubby privet hedge.

When I first heard his name, I wondered whether he had any connection with Sandt Street, maybe a remote cousin or descendant of the original gentleman? But after a good look at this dilapidated old man, the thought faded. Still, I was curious, and one day I asked one of the girls who worked in the Big House. And she told me. And wow. And now I have to switch to another subject.

Generally speaking Mother left our fates (mine and Peedo's) in God's care. On the other hand, here I was, a couple of years out of high school, and college was still nowhere in sight. There was no money. Was God napping? Maybe, sort of. Sometimes she put God in the same category as Uncle George, who had been a drummer boy in the War, and had actually beat his drum at the Battle of Shiloh, but now couldn't tell you which side he had been on. In other words, God sometimes got confused like Uncle George. God's heart was in the right place, and He loved you, but sometimes He got mixed up, and then you had to step in and take charge.

Now Mother was a very saintly woman, but I was not a saintly youth, and her visions of my professional potentials were completely askew. Nevertheless she brought pressure on certain authority figures at Southwest Bible College, and they gave me a scholarship – to take two courses – at night. The arrangement was conditioned on the premise that I would forget chemistry and that I would work toward a B.D. – Bachelor of Divinity. It was a ministerial scholarship. It was a mistake.

I was finally in college. I was nineteen years old.

The two courses were English 11 and Bible 11. English 11 was a breeze, but I had trouble with Bible 11, like, was the world really created on a Friday morning in 4,004 B.C.?

But I played the game. I didn't argue with our Bible professor, Dr. Mord. I wasn't going to risk my scholarship. I even wrote a model sermon on how Joshua lifted up his arms, made the sun stand still, and got a giant cactus named after him.

Dr. Mord was tall, gaunt, with bleak cheeks and sunken eyes. His mouth always seemed compressed. He spoke, walked, and taught his course with strong presence and authority. He was subtle, brilliant.

During my first class in Bible 11 it occurred to me that I had met Professor Mord before – or at least I had seen him somewhere. His face was . . . troubling. It was not exactly evil, but there was something wrong with it. It was incomplete. It lacked something, some quality or trait that would certify its possessor as human. Where had I encountered him? Nothing came to mind. The mystery gradually became a tantalizing unscratchable itch.

He had a peculiar fame. He had worked with William Jennings Bryan at the Scopes Monkey Trial in Tennessee in 1925, where he had helped the Great Commoner prepare for cross-examination by Clarence Darrow.

Some of his more famous sermons had been collected and published in bound calf-leather with gilt title (courtesy of the Texas Purity League, of which he was sometime president), *The Sword of Christ*. The lead sermon explained why just about everybody was going to Hell.

He was a Fundamentalist. He took the Bible literally.

It was rumored that he had once seriously proposed to sail to England for the sole purpose of urinating on the grave of Charles Darwin, and that he had called the trip off only when he learned that Darwin was inaccessibly and inexplicably interred in Westminster Abbey.

He and I were doing fine until the last week of the spring semester. "For your term paper," he said, "give me a sermon based on a biblical text of your choice. And illustrate your text with a real-life experience."

What I gave him was the story of Bernard Sandt, the old man in the rocking chair. And my text? Ecclesiastes 10:1, "Cast your bread upon the waters, and after many days it will return to you."

Bernard Sandt was born and raised in Fort West in affluence. Before and during the War he made millions in Chile nitrate, "caliche," for fertilizer for gunpowder, for nitric acid. He married a society girl and said goodbye to his mistress, Diana Mulligan, an actress. He gave her $25,000 as a parting gift. He was also charitable in other ways. He gave money to the Bible College, to the church, to St. Joseph's Sanctuary, to anyone who asked. When the Public Library needed supplemental income to meet its 1917 payroll, he set up the Sandt Fund. There was a famous picture in the *Star-Telegram,* where he and Miss Scather, the Librarian, are holding hands. He was on every charity hit list.

Then came the crash of '29.

Now, even during the worst of the Depression there was still a market for nitrates, and he might have survived on a reduced scale except for a man he had never met: Fritz Haber.

Haber was a great German chemist. He had invented a process for making nitrates from atmospheric nitrogen. Badische, the German chemical giant, had built a nitrate plant for him at Oppau, near Magdeburg. Hydrogen and nitrogen were reacted in the presence of a catalyst, under heat and pressure, and that gave ammonia, which was then oxidized to nitric acid, which was reacted with more ammonia, to form ammonium nitrate. And so on to potassium nitrate and gunpowder. Haber's process had kept Germany in the War for an extra three years, and after the War his nitrates flooded the world market. His synthetic nitrate was far cheaper than caliche from Chile. Chilean nitrate couldn't compete, and Sandt was soon bankrupt, destroyed by nitrogen molecules in the air over Oppau.

He lost everything, money, wife, house, the works. In the fall of 1930, when financiers were jumping out of Wall Street windows, Bernard Sandt was down and out, penniless, and actually hungry. He managed to get to Fort West. He applied for work at the Bible College. Couldn't they use a grounds keeper? No deal. It wouldn't look right, they said. Next, the church. No, again it wouldn't look right. Then to the Public Library. He could dust off books, maybe sleep on a mat in the cellar? "Oh, poor Mr. Sandt," said Miss Scather, "it would break my heart to have to see you in that degraded condition every day. Please go away."

On the evening of Good Friday, 1930, Mr. Sandt, like a jester-less King Lear, found himself trudging along East Second Street. His storm-wracked heath was the T & P spur that centered the street. He was going to catch a freight headed . . . anywhere. All he could think was, get out of town.

Now, as he walked slowly past the Big House, Diana Mulligan was sweeping the front porch and getting ready for the Easter weekend trade. She looked up, but just gave him a passing glance. Another bum on the way to the big freight yard. But then she stopped sweeping and looked again. Something vaguely familiar? An old customer, maybe? The sun was on the back of his head. She couldn't get a good look at his face.

"Jesus," she muttered. "No. It can't be. Jesus God."

She whistled a certain tune: Bach's *Sheep May Safely Graze.*

He took two steps. Stopped, shrugged, then took another step. The tune didn't go away. He looked over toward the porch and squinted, and now they could see each other.

"Di?" he sort of croaked.

"Bunny!" she shrieked. She ran down into the street, and you would have thought they were both crazy, the way they cried and whooped and hollered and carried on.

She brought him in and personally bathed him in her private tub and got him some clean clothes, and broke out her private stock of Black Label and had William get the sirloin from the ice-box and grill it exactly medium rare.

Mr. Sandt went to sleep right after supper, and William carried him up to her bed.

He's been there at the Big House ever since, rocking in his chair on the porch, smoking his Prince Albert, and once in a while he gets up to spit over the railing into the scrubby privet hedge.

This explains about everything except how the street got its name. She did it, of course. In 1919 she paid good money to various members of the City Council, and the ordinance was duly voted, passed, and recorded. She also paid for making and installing the street signs. That's why the name SANDT is twice as big as other street signs in Fort West, bigger even than Robt E Lee (South Side) and Houston (downtown).

That was Mr. Bernard Sandt's story, and that was the guts of my term paper for Dr. Mord. Cast your bread upon the waters, and after many days it will return to you. Sandt gave Diana Mulligan $25,000, and with that, and the help of God, she created the Red Light District in Fort West. Sandt cast his bread upon the waters, and his investment paid off. In his hour of need, when his former friends and beneficiaries had rejected and humiliated him, God led him back to Madame Diana Mulligan.

So what happened to my magnificent sermon?

Black Witches

Dr. Mord had asked me to come by after class that night, and he would give me his comments in person. That was fine with me.

I sat in his office and watched him with gleaming eyes as he silently read my masterpiece, my *tour de force,* slowly, page by page. I knew it was a terrific sermon. It had drama. It had a clear moral lesson. It had familiar local color. Dr. Mord would surely nominate this little beauty for the Annual Southwest Sermon Competition.

Finally he laid the carefully typed sheets on his desk and turned to me. His eyes were dark bottomless holes, such as you might find in a bare skull. His thin face held no expression.

For the first time I sensed that all might not be well.

"Joseph," he said slowly, "I will put the matter plainly. Your alleged sermon not only recommends and supports whoring, it sanctifies it with holy writ. I do not judge Bernard Sandt. Evidently he was seduced by that evil woman. Oh, sad, sad. The problem, Joseph, is that *you* are unable to perceive this. A man with the true calling would actually be able to *smell* it." He sniffed.

I wanted to ask him what it smelled like, but I didn't dare.

He considered me grimly. "Joseph, you are an agent of Satan. An unwitting agent, perhaps, but his servant none the less. You are evil. Fortunately, we found you out in time." With slow ceremonial strokes (each the cry of a soul in purgatory) he tore up my sermon and dropped the pieces in his waste basket. "You flunk Bible 11. Your scholarship cannot be renewed, of course. I will pray for you. Now get out."

And now, when I thought my life had hit utter nadir, it fell still further.

His desk lamp lit his face from below, like Bela Lugosi in *Dracula.* There was a sudden tic in his right eye, like an involuntary wink.

That did it. I had sudden total recall. I knew where I had seen him before. I know you, Dr. Mord. I know the wink, the burning eyes, the grin. You are the phosphorus face on Mrs. Gruen's wall. You are grinning Hell. You are Lucifer.

I got out. I started walking.

As I walked into the night I was thinking, this is bad, very bad. I was walking, but my feet didn't seem to have any sensation: they had no contact with the grass. In fact, I was numb all over. I started down University Boulevard in a daze.

Finally, one by one, my senses began to click back on. Touch. Sight. Sound. I noted that my legs (good old horse!) had, by rote and reflex, taken me safely through the darkness and into Forest Park, my usual route home.

I stopped and looked around. There was a sudden flash off to the west. Sheet lightning. For a moment the Park entrance looked like a Gustave Doré engraving of the Gates of Hell, back-lit, brooding, sinister. Abandon all hope, ye who enter.

I groaned. My chances for college – gone . . . even night classes . . . and Mother had worked so hard to get me that scholarship. Money. $14 a week will barely buy beans. Everything is money. She will be crushed. I've got to get back into school.

I took stock of the situation. I had been working for the paper company for nearly three years without a raise. Two or three times a week at noon break I changed into my good clothes and made the rounds of the employment agencies. No luck.

I needed somebody to talk to . . . somebody to tell me I'm at least half-way decent . . . that there is hope for me yet . . . that thoughts of suicide are premature.

Cybele, oh Cybele . . .

I walked down into the Park.

Forest Park, a twenty-acre semi-wilderness, was a short-cut between the Bible College and home. The Park had a tiny zoo (complete with ancient lion), picnic areas with benches and grills, a merry-go-round, and lots of trees – oaks, maples, sycamores. Little asphalt paths interlaced the central areas, and here and there an arc light made stark shadows of the trees.

It was about 10:30, and the lion was roaring. That meant a storm was coming. An unwelcome final touch to a bad evening. I looked overhead. Pitch dark. But I knew the big thunderhead was there, winding up. This one would be short but savage. On down the path, beyond the arc light, there was a storage shed, with bundles of hay. Potential shelter. I quickened my steps.

As the path rounded a little bend, I saw a figure – a woman – sitting on the bench under the light. I stopped, startled. There was something magical here. I thought of Rima, the forest naiad in Hudson's *Green Mansions.*

She looked up, and now we could see each other's faces.

"Cybele!" I gasped. Not Miss Wilson. Not Miss Cybele.

I had called her by her Christian name. Right away I knew, and she must have known, that I was no longer the boy of her high school chemistry class. I was twenty, she was twenty-seven.

I was telling her that henceforward we would be on a first-name basis, practically contemporaries.

"Joe!" She stood up. We studied each other under the glare-light. In the years since high school she had grown even more beautiful.

I spoke first. "What are you doing here?"

She laughed. "I could ask you the same thing. Okay, I'm here for the noctuids."

Just then something with wings – a bat? – no, not a bat – circled her head, then lighted delicately on her outstretched hand. It must have had a six-inch wingspread.

"A moth?" I asked softly. She nodded. I watched as the beautiful creature probed at the little cotton ball in her palm. I assumed it was soaked in sugar water. Two tiny eyes shone up at me, reflecting the overhead light. Odd. Very few moths have reflecting eyes. "Black witch?" I hazarded.

She chuckled. "I see you still read."

A second winged creature joined the first. They seemed to argue about who could sit where. Then a third.

I took a deep breath. There was a subtle scent . . . hers.

I thought back. I had read something somewhere. There was a strong chemical, with a funny name: *bombykol.* One molecule can bring in the male moth from a mile away. "You have a dermal pheromone?" I said. "You exude a sexual attractant?"

"Yes. Unusual, but not unknown. It's essence of bluebonnet, an analog of *bombykol.* Nicholas Guppy, the English botanist, had something similar. He had to fight off the butterflies whenever he went out into the fields."

"Three hundred years ago in any civilized country they would have burnt you at the stake."

"Quite likely. And even today, some people would be very upset. I can turn it on and off. Right now it's on." She grinned and held up her left hand. "Care for a closer smell?"

I knew then that a wonderful new life was starting, for me, for her, for us together. In true cavalier fashion, I bowed and kissed her hand.

I felt a drop of water on my head. Still holding her hand, I looked up. First things first. "Cybele, it's going to storm. We have to get out of here."

"I –"

Off behind us there was a sudden brilliant flash, then a deafening crash that echoed and re-echoed, then the slow anguished shriek of a falling tree. It seemed very close.

I looked at her. There was a brief stark vision of Cybele Wilson staring at me, white-faced, wide-eyed, mouth open, and then the overhead arc light crackled and everything was pitch-black. I fumbled in the dark, grabbed her, and started pulling her down the path toward the shed. She seemed paralyzed. I picked her up and carried her. A tree fell just behind us. Hailstones pelted us as I ran, some as big as golf balls.

We were lucky. It was a miraculous passage. I didn't stumble. And it was weird. On that freighted journey to the hay shed I was smelling her body, and I was thinking – *pheromone* – from the Greek, *pherein,* to carry, and *horman,* to excite. Prophetic.

We lay down together in the shed among the broken hay bales, silent, just listening to the storm. It was all around us.

My shirt had slipped up. She ran her hand over my bare chest. I thought of the aborted rendezvous with the doomed Sally Winters. This time it would be different. She said, "You're not even breathing hard."

"It wasn't very far. Why are we whispering?"

She chuckled. It was a throaty thing. I noted then that I was lying part-way over her body, with one hand on her hip. She had one free hand, and now it was resting on the back of my neck. Except for flashes of lightning through cracks in the door, it was totally dark inside the shed.

"Cybele?" I said.

She was silent, and motionless.

"I love you," I said. "Kiss me."

Her grip around my neck tightened. She sighed and pulled my face down to hers. After a moment we fumbled around in the dark. She got her underpants off and gathered her skirt up around her hips while I unbuttoned my fly and got rid of my britches and shorts.

More fumbling. She used her hands to help me enter her, and then pulled hard on my buttocks. I thrust hard. She gasped as though in sharp pain, and then there was this long sigh. I had breached her hymen. There would probably be blood. Let it be so.

Our orgasms were immediate and simultaneous. We lay in each other's arms for a few minutes. Then she sat up, I helped her strip away her dress and slip, then her brassiere. In the dim occasional light I could see her breasts, hanging in structured cones. I cupped them in my hands, I kissed the hard nipples. She put her arms around my back and I hovered over her once more.

Making love to Cybele that night . . . to say what it was like, I can give only a vulgar comparison: you can't eat just one peanut. We would think we were through, drained, exhausted. And then I would touch her, and her nipples would harden again, our lips would search . . . fasten . . .

I tried to memorize her body, but it was too protean. One moment her pubic hair was a polychrome fluorescence, then the next a diffuse ray of moonlight would show golden-edged fibers. Even as I licked her underarms, the taste of her perspiration changed from sea-brine to nectar.

The signals that her legs sent as they devoured my body seemed to shift moment by moment.

And throughout, I drowned drunkenly in the sea of her perfume.

It occurred to me that it wasn't wine that Circe used on Ulysses and his men – it was *scent.* I thought of Poe's "To Helen", the Nicean barks on the perfumed sea, carrying the weary way-worn traveler home.

And in between, I was thinking. I thought about a lot of things.

She was older than I. She gave me that gift of years. I had neither earned it nor deserved it. She gave it freely, and I took it. For us the age difference was irrelevant. On the fields of Eros we met as equals.

It was a long night, it was a short night. I don't know when the storm quit. It couldn't have lasted very long. When we opened the shed door the moon and stars were clearly visible. We sat on a bale of hay and looked out through the doorway. We talked a long time.

This thing about lovers being able to read each other's thoughts . . . only partly true. She could read all of mine. I could read only some of hers. It would have to do.

I said (no preamble . . . she would either know or not know): "Was that your portrait?"

"The girl with the cup. Yes. I knew you were there. I asked Edith to hang it. I didn't want you to forget me."

"The cup . . . what did that signify?"

She hesitated. "I . . . it's sort of a symbol . . . a covenant . . . it says love is forever."

Translation: if she knew, she didn't want to talk about it. Again, fine with me.

I had thought I had had a bad time with Dr. Mord until I learned how she had wound up *her* school year. Maybe that's why we were together that night. We needed each other.

"I used our old Ford coil set-up," she said, "except that instead of air, I used a mixture of methane, ammonia, hydrogen, and water vapor. I added a little phosphate to the water, plus a sort of catalyst. I wanted to duplicate the atmosphere of the early Earth, before there were any plants, and no free oxygen. The sparks would simulate lightning."

I was thinking, trying to visualize the organics. "You'd get formaldehyde, ammonia, HCN . . . "

"Right."

"You'd need glycine?"

"Keep going."

"You'd probably get some aminonitrile . . . yeah, and *that* would hydrolyze to glycine."

She grinned. "Right."

"So then what happened?"

"Well, by the second day the product began to cloud up. On the fourth morning scum was floating on the surface. I pulled a sample. My analysis wasn't complete, but I found some components of deoxyribonucleic acid, including adenine and thymine, not to mention several additional amino acids – alanine, valine, proline, sarcosine, all well-known cell products.

"On the morning of the fifth day I could see that – *something* – had happened. The surface scum had disappeared. The broth was clear except for some odd brown specks in suspension, iotas barely visible to the eye. Dozens of them, moving, Joe, swimming, *cavorting.*"

I thought of Genesis 1:20, "Let the waters bring forth swarms of living creatures . . . And there was evening and there was morning, a fifth day." "Life?" I whispered. "Cybele, did you make *life? "*And why, I thought, should she not? Why shouldn't Cybele, Goddess of Nature, make all the damn life she wanted?

She didn't answer.

I persisted. "You said you used a catalyst. What was it?"

"When I took out the samples for analysis, I deliberately breathed on the broth."

Of course, I thought. Genesis 2:7, ". . . then the Lord God formed man of dust from the ground, and breathed into his nostrils the breath of life; and man became a living being." "Go on," I said. I hardly recognized my own voice.

She continued softly. "Rumors began to float around, mostly false. The *Star-Telegram* sent around a reporter with a cameraman. Mr. Vachel turned them away. They were going to print something anyhow but Mr. Vachel called Amon Carter and got the piece killed. They had already set the head, 'High-school teacher creates life.' "

"It would have been quite a story." I put my hand on her bare knee.

She put a hand on mine. "Indeed. Mr. Vachel was upset. He demanded that I dismantle the equipment. We argued. No decision. But when I came in next morning, I found that the whole thing had been destroyed. Broken glass all over the place. The product was splattered all over everything. Your Ford coil was gone. Mr. Vachel was not sympathetic. The faculty was like a family, he said. We have to get along. I didn't seem to be able to fit in."

"They didn't renew your contract?"

"No."

I didn't know what to say. We got up and walked barefoot outside the shed. We stared out into the moonlit night, Adam and Eve in halcyon pre-apple Eden. At first the only sound was the intermittent arrhythmia of residual rainwater dripping from leaves. Then, as our hearing sharpened, the nocturnal susurrus came back on in volume: playful breezes in the trees, crickets calling for mates or maybe just feeling happy, far away a dog barking in counterpoint to the rumble of a distant truck. We were quiet for a while.

Cybele pointed overhead. The moon appeared surrounded by a luminous ring. "Ah!" she murmured. "A paraselene, caused by water vapor in the stratosphere." She laughed softly. "A propitious sign. The gods look upon us with favor!"

The gods, I thought, are probably shocked out of their godly gourds by what they have seen tonight. I held her close to my side.

I wanted to ask her a million questions. Why had she chosen chemistry? How had she financed it? Who and where were her parents, her family? How had she known about the job at Mongolia? Why had she been in that cave by Sycamore Creek? What had happened there? But I sensed that the time was not ripe for her to talk about these things. Her virgin blood was a magic talisman that silenced me.

Something flitted by my shoulder and hovered near her face.

She chuckled. "A black witch. They probably wondered what happened to me. And there's another." I turned her back toward the shed.

"It's after midnight. We'd better get dressed."

"Yeah."

I tried a question. "How did you know I would be here?"

"I knew."

Yes, she knew. We had lines, parts in a drama that had opened years ago in a cave in Sycamore Park. What else did she know? Did she know how it would end?

I knew only that we were part of each other.

In days to come we made love. We talked. We made love. We held hands in long silences. We made love. We made love in her apartment; in her car; once in a cheap motel. And like furtive teenagers, in the darkened balconies of movie theaters. In rest rooms. Once in a stuck elevator.

Necessity bred strange geometries. There is a contorted statue by Rodin, *L'Eternel Printemps*, in the Metropolitan Museum of Art, in New York. The woman is in total abandon, the bodies are dissolved into each other, like a chemical reaction. Even so, compared to us his lovers were but fumbling dilettantes.

Gradually she became demanding, hungry, almost fierce. Her kisses sometimes drew blood. Her embraces became clutches, as though she would totally merge her body with mine. As though each tryst was the last, and she had to store up memories to last an eternity.

We had earnest conversations. We reproached; we remonstrated. We made promises.

Me: One day you'll leave me.

She: Would you like that?

Me: How can you ask? Shame!

She: You want me to stay with you forever?

Me: Yes.

She: You're *sure?*

Me: Yes.

She: All right then. I'll never leave you. I'll be with you forever and ever.

Sometimes we talked of more practical matters.

"You'll need another scholarship," she said. "I'll talk to some people I know at Southern Christian. And you ought to get a better job – something with more money. I can give you some names. And never forget chemistry. You can do it."

Fingerprints

On a tip from Diana Mulligan I left the paper company and took a job as a fingerprint clerk in the Fort West Police Department. Dame Mulligan had friends – or at least contacts – within the Department, deriving, I presumed, from intermittent raids and/or calls to quell disturbances. Of course, she had known I was out there looking for a better job, so her help was entirely natural and believable. The odd thing was, when I told Cybele, she just smiled and asked a few perfunctory questions. As though maybe she had already known. A puzzle. I put it out of my head.

I loved the job. Number one, it paid twice my wages at the paper company; number two, it opened doors to an exciting new world. Number three, they put me on an evening shift, three to eleven, which meant I could go to Southern Christian in the daytime. But I still couldn't take chemistry, because the labs were in the afternoon, when I had to be at work.

I fingerprinted people, the innocent, the guilty. Men, women, children, all ages, all colors. Living, dead.

I worked in the photo darkroom. I took mug shots. I printed the negatives and pressed the positive prints on waxed ferrotins, where they popped off, one by one, at irregular intervals, like popcorn.

I typed letters – to J. Edgar Hoover; to the D.A.; to police chiefs in other towns. I took down confessions in shorthand from exhausted men and women and from frightened boys. I knew the odor of human fear.

Yes, I remember especially the odors, the hypo and acetic acid in the darkroom, the daily Lysol swabbings in the cells.

The Police Department had its own rules. Like chess, its rules were complicated, but had a sort of internal consistency. The P.D. was in fact as beautiful as chess, once you survived the initial hazing.

A favorite trick was to put eggwhite in a condom, seal the condom with a rubber band, and put the thing in a pocket of the victim's jacket hanging in the side rack. I found it by accident. They probably wondered what explanation I could give my mother, or my girl friend, or classmates at SCU. So did I. I tossed it in the toilet, and after that I always checked my belongings before I went off duty.

A favorite: I might be telling a story to three detectives, about a thing that had happened at the Big House or at the paper company. One by one they would turn and walk away. Half way through, I was left talking to myself. Actually, I was too surprised to feel humiliated.

I learned slowly.

Sometimes I fought back.

They knew I had classes at SCU in the morning. I think it made them uneasy. Not jealous . . . just uneasy, uncomfortable. None of them had ever been to college. It was simply irrelevant to earning a living. Some hadn't even finished high school. But they could sense that things were changing.

I stacked my school texts by my jacket every afternoon I came to work. Schultz, one of the older detectives, noted I was studying French.

Detective Irwin Schultz was highly respected. Still, he was a crab. He seemed to be mad at nearly everybody nearly all the time. And the newer you were in the Department, the more he picked on you. I tried to stay out of his way.

His attitude was, if not justified, at least understandable. For Life had mocked, cheated, and generally frustrated him. Three years earlier he had caught a couple of bullets in a liquor raid and had almost got his name engraved on the silver plaque in Chief Stahl's office, reserved for men who had fallen in the line of duty. His wounds had put him in the hospital for several weeks, and while he lay on his back in the City-County in bitter contemplation, the exam for lieutenant was held.

Anyhow, one evening when I walked into the ready room to check the blotter I noted that Schultz and a couple of other detectives and uniforms were hovering around a card table in the corner and were busy with coffee and doughnuts. A couple of the men were further engaged in an attempt to ignite sugar cubes with a burning match. Interesting. I had read about it somewhere. You can't simply hold the match flame to the lump of sugar and expect it to catch fire. No. There's a trick. But none of them knew the trick, and so one by one they all gave up.

Schultz was last. He scowled and gave a quarter to one of the men. Evidently he had bet twenty-five cents he could light the sugar lump. He turned, saw me, and probably assumed I was enjoying his discomfort. Actually, I didn't care how he felt.

He smiled. It was a sort of knowing, wicked smile. "Joe," he said, "you can help us. We've pulled in this Frenchie, from Paris, France. He don't speak English. We need his name, where he lives, and when he's going back to France. You're studying French. Can you ask him?"

A nondescript looking man stepped from behind Schultz.

Schultz flicked a glance toward his partner, Ebbitts.

Ben Ebbitts was the perfect partner for Schultz — the only living creature Schultz wasn't perpetually mad at. Sort of a shadow, or carbon copy. Sharks have pilot fish; Schultz had a trailing fish. Long association and deathless devotion had implanted in the younger detective Schultz's same expressions, same voice intonations, same stride, arm and body motions, and so on. When Schultz spoke, Ebbitts's lips moved slightly, in diminutive imitation of the master's speech. Schultz wore Ebbitts the way a woman wears a matching accessory, like a hat, or scarf, or handbag. Neither was aware of this. Achilles and Patroclus would have understood it.

And just now senior and junior exchanged a look loaded with meaning.

Something was wrong. Aside from the question of a Frenchman in the middle of Texas knowing no English.

I started out slowly. I said to the alleged Frenchman, *"Comment vous appellez-vous?"* How do you call yourself?

He grimaced, waved his hands, opened his mouth, and a torrent came forth. I didn't understand a word of it. He and Schultz exchanged looks.

Okay, it was a set-up. I frowned, turned to the detective. "I'm having trouble with one of the verbs."

"Yeah?" His eyes gleamed. He saw he had me.

"One way he says, 'Schultz *has* a big prick.' The other way, 'Schultz *is* a big prick.' "

They all stared at me. Jaws dropped. Schultz turned various colors. He glanced at his Gallic stoolie, who cringed and started backing away. "No, Irwin! I swear! He's lying!"

The three left together, washed away by laughter. As I have mentioned, the P.D. loves a good joke.

How to win friends.

As it turned out, Schultz wasn't done with me. I had merely stimulated him.

Scene Two:

His cousin Earl the well digger had dug a well for one of the uniforms, a mild-mannered older man named Max Russell. The well was on Max's farm in Johnson County, where Max would be retiring in a couple of years. It was a deep well, because Johnson County is subject to severe intermittent droughts and the extra depth is needed not only to tap additional aquifers but also for water storage.

Storage was the question Max brought to me, followed by an irate Schultz. Earl had guaranteed 300 gallons of storage. The question: had he met his guarantee?

Max explained, with frequent interruptions from Schultz. "The well is 8 inches in diameter and 130 feet deep. There's 90 feet of standing water in the well. So how many gallons is that?"

"Obviously, way over the guarantee," growled Schultz. "And Earl ought to know. He's been spudding wells for twenty years."

I pulled a little device from my shirt pocket.

"What's *that?*" Schultz demanded suspiciously. "What are you doing?"

"Slide rule. Only six inches, but it's well-machined, and will give us three significant figures. I adjusted the slide. The answer is 235 gallons."

There was a long silence. They looked at me, then at each other, then back at me. I wondered, what is going on here? What's wrong? I learned all this stuff in the seventh grade, at Bagley Junior High. The slide rule I got at Woolworth's for ten cents, instructions included.

Schultz glowered. "Well, that's just plain wrong. Earl knows what he's doing. He knows his own work. You gonna prance around with a toy like that and then tell him he's a liar?"

"Joe," Max said reasonably, "explain how you did it. Put it down on paper. Okay?"

"Sure. First, we get the volume in cubic feet. That's cross section times depth. Cross section is *pi* r square. *Pi* is 3.1416. R is 4 inches, or 1/3 foot. R square is 1/3 times 1/3, or 1/9. Depth is 90." I wrote it down. "The 9's cancel . . . so . . . and that gives you the volume in cubic feet, *pi* times 10, or 31.4 cubic feet of standing water. Now, 1 cubic foot of water is 7.48

gallons so 31.4 cubic feet is 31.4 times 7.48, or 235 gallons." I handed Max the piece of paper. He beamed at me as though I had given him the winning ticket to the Irish sweepstakes.

"Nah, you screwed up somewhere," scowled Schultz. "That ought to be *three* thirty-five."

They left together, still arguing. I heard later that Earl redug the well, no cost.

I had this remarkable talent for making friends and enemies simultaneously.

I thought about Max's well. There would be a windmill and a big wooden tank, just like our windmill in Colorado City when I was a boy. And the wind blowing, and the vanes whirling, and the pump rods cranking away. Especially the wind. As the local poet said,

> Blows like this for days at a spell.
> Rest of the time it blows like hell.

I felt homesick.

My affair with Cybele swept on unabated through the winter and into the spring. We made love in some strange places. Once in an empty church. Once in a field of bluebonnets. Several times in the midnight paths of Forest Park. I knew her body better than I knew my own.

We never used a condom. "You'll get pregnant," I warned.

"No."

I let it go. She knew her cycles; I didn't.

I suggested marriage. She refused even to discuss it.

One evening we saw a strange movie together: *Death Takes a Holiday*, with Fredric March as Death and Evelyn Venable as Grazia, who falls in love with him. This was a re-run. Cybele had seen it two years earlier, and she insisted now that I see it. I think she was trying to use March's lines to explain something to me. "To come with me can be a beautiful thing. I open the door to wonders you cannot imagine."

Oh yeah? The problem here is, you right away encounter the human reaction – everybody wants to go to heaven, but nobody wants to die . . . not just yet, anyhow. And if Death offered such an attractive deal, how come that theme music, Sibelius's *Valse Triste?* So beautiful, so mournful, it brought tears to my eyes, and to hers.

As though to compound the effect, she had bought the record, a twelve-inch platter, and in her apartment we rolled up the little rug, and we danced to the most melancholy waltz in the history of dance or of music.

But if she was trying to tell me death (lower case!) could be beautiful, the effort was a total flop. The record came to an end and shut off.

"It's ten-thirty," I said. "I'm on the midnight shift tonight. Gotta go."
I held her close to me. She nestled under my chin.

"Yes." Her voice was low, uncertain.

We should never have gone to that damn movie. I took her by the shoulders. "What's wrong?"

"Nothing." She laughed and stepped away. "Come on, help me roll the rug back."

We did this with expert nudges of our toes. At the finish she said, very casually, "I have to go away for a week or so."

I didn't react at first. What I thought she had said made absolutely no sense. She couldn't have said it. I repeated the words in my mind. She *had* said it.

I jerked. Chills ran up and down my arms. I got my breathing under control and studied her calm, graven face, like the queens of ancient Egypt, serene in ivory. In the movie Grazia had looked into the face of Death, and had seen beauty. I now looked into the face of beauty, and I saw Death. I grabbed her by the shoulders and we studied each other. I sort of croaked, "What the hell are you talking about? Go away? Why? Where? For how long?"

"Ah, Joe. It's just a few days. I wish I could tell you everything, but actually, I don't know. Please, we'll talk later. Just now, you'd better go on to work. Kiss me."

And so I did. I trailed a thin wraith of her scent behind me on the way to my car. One might think that I would eventually become immune to it, that I would develop some sort of protective olfactory paralysis. But in fact, the change in sensitivity went in the other direction. A solitary molecule could open my mnemonic floodgates, as it did now, so that I could not possibly feel annoyed with her. With myself, perhaps, but not with her. Never.

As I drove to work, I sensed that this was part of her secret drama, with scenes she knew, but I didn't. "Why? Where? For how long?" It was probably true, as she claimed, she didn't have all the answers.

A week later I got a strange phone call at work. It was a few minutes after eleven at night, the evening shift, and I was on my way out.

"Joe?"

"Yes?"

"This is Di Mulligan. Do you remember me?"

"Di? Of course I remember you. What's up?"

"I'm calling from Harris Hospital."

"Oh? Harris . . ." I couldn't seem to get the situation in focus.

"Cybele . . . just out of recovery . . . she was in surgery for four hours . . ."

Di sounded very tired. And obviously she had been crying.

I came to life. "Is she okay?"

"She keeps asking for you. Joe, can you come?"

"I'm on the way."

As I rattled along in my ancient Chevy roadster, all I could think of was questions, questions.

What was Di Mulligan to Cybele? Why had my beloved never mentioned Di? And thinking way back, how had Cybele known about the job opening at Mongolia? Okay, now I knew. Di had told her, of course. They had talked. They were intimate. And they had probably conspired together to get my interview for this job in the P.D. Had Cybele once been one of Di's girls? No. It didn't make any sense.

Di stood up when I entered the little semi-private room. Her makeup was streaked and mottled, as though haphazardly repaired after a general demolition. We touched hands briefly, then I went over to the bed.

Cybele's eyes opened, closed, opened again. I bent over and kissed her on the cheek. The odor of anesthetic hit me like a hammer. She spoke in a soft guttural. "Joe, mother."

By then it was no surprise. I had a handle on the situation. I said gravely, "A pleasure, ma'am."

"We didn't want you to know," Di said in a dead monotone.

"You were wrong."

"Yeah, maybe . . . but . . . you know . . . trouble at school . . . trouble everywhere . . ."

"No. It's okay." I turned back to Cybele. "Sweetheart, Di and I are going out into the hall for a minute. We'll be right back."

Outside, I took Di's hands. I looked into her bloodshot eyes. "I want to know everything."

She sighed, looked down. "Cancer," she said dully. "Renal cancer. They took out the kidney, but it was too late."

I swallowed hard. "How long has she got?"

She looked up at me with dark brown eyes that said everything, and nothing. Once she must have been a very beautiful woman. She lowered her eyes again as though they were a burden too heavy to lift. She didn't answer.

It was wrong to keep after her, but I did. "Di, how long?"

She lifted the words out, one at a time. "We're taking her home . . . tomorrow afternoon." (Long pause.) "Can you come and see her once in a while?"

"Oh . . . Di!" We hugged. She was through crying. I provided the tears.

Miss Scather

I spent the night at the hospital and most of the next morning. Di scolded me. "Look, you can't do anything here. You're soon due at work." She studied me. "Oh, Joe, you look godawful. Go home, shave, change your shirt. We'll take her home this afternoon. Let her rest a little. You can see her tomorrow.?

"Yes."

So I went on to work. I had hardly hung up my jacket when Chief of Detectives Goodall called me into his office. He looked unhappy, but resigned. "Mr. Barnes, Miss Scather, Texas Purity League."

My heartbeat doubled for a moment. Adrenalin began to flow, my right ear tingled. I nodded politely. "Ma'am."

She looked at me curiously, perhaps wondering if she had ever seen me before.

She had, but it was a long time ago.

This was how. I was twelve years old. I had a "lab" in a ramshackle shed in our backyard, and I wanted to make gunpowder.

I had a hard time finding the recipe. The Fort West Public Library didn't seem to have any books that explained specifically how to make gunpowder. The upstairs juvenile section had a few science and chemistry books, but the then librarian, Miss Scather, had carefully excluded all "upstairs" books that mentioned sex and gunpowder. In fact, anything at all that might tend to corrupt innocent young minds.

Oh, they had a lot of interesting juvenilia: Terhune's books about collies, novels about the naval academy, and actually some rather dramatic stuff about early Texas history, all about how the bad Mexicans maltreated our noble Texas ancestors.

But nothing on gunpowder.

The library had other glaring deficiencies. Not only did it lack a formulary book for explosives, it didn't even have the Tarzan books. Listen to this (the boy Tarzan has just killed a horrid gorilla). "As the body rolled to the ground Tarzan of the Apes placed his foot upon the neck of his life-long enemy, and raising his eyes to the full moon threw back his fierce young head and voiced the wild and terrible cry of his people." You can bet Miss Scather wasn't going to let *that* get past her!

Irene Scather, our Public Librarian, was probably about fifty years old, tall, broad, heavy. In those early years whenever I looked at her I thought of an army tank – an immense behemoth, implacable, irresistible. I was certain that (if she so chose) she could crash through brick walls without bruising knuckles or nose.

In one of my musings about God I sometimes wondered, suppose He got into an argument with her. Who would win? Of course, He was God Almighty, and all-powerful, and so on, but then here was this invincible female *tank,* loaded with artillery and machine guns, grenades, whatever tanks have, plus guile and full knowledge in the ways of her opposition. Interesting question. God had better think twice before he tangled with Irene Scather!

In those days it was obvious to me that our Guardian of the Books was really just a part of a wide, subterranean conspiracy, joined in by family, school, and the State of Texas, and devoted to the proposition that boys would be permitted to know only certain things, these and no others.

It was a conspiracy worthy of my metal (as John Carter of the Mars books would say), and I fought back, with stealth and low cunning. Oh, Miss Scather and I never actually declared war. Outright confrontations were rare, because I could always hear her coming. Except that once.

Actually, I finally found what I needed upstairs in a book about the Civil War. (And I wasn't even looking for it. I simply read a lot.) Potassium nitrate was in short supply, and somebody was trying to persuade Abe Lincoln to switch to potassium chlorate. So there it was, in black and white. I felt like Keats's Cortez (actually it was Balboa), on his peak in Darien, looking out over the Pacific with a wild surmise. Charcoal plus sulfur plus either potassium nitrate or potassium chlorate equals gunpowder.

And the book even explained why the Union army decided not to use the chlorate: it corroded gun barrels. No problem. I didn't have a gun.

Everything was available at the corner drug store. I saved my lunch money and bought samples. I mixed up little spoonfuls, some with KNO_3, some with $KClO_3$. I discovered that mixtures with nitrate burned slowly, those with chlorate much faster. I decided to concentrate on potassium chlorate.

The day came when I very carefully mixed up a sizable heap of equal amounts of chlorate, sulfur, and charcoal. It was Saturday, in mid-June, not a cloud in a very blue sky, already very hot, about 95 outside, maybe 105 in my lab. I didn't mind at all. I had four quart-size Mason jars standing by. As soon as I tested my mixture, I was going to store it safely away, pending use, say in firecrackers, paper cartouches to put on the streetcar tracks, home-made Roman candles, and so on. Save a lot for the Fourth of July.

My boyhood lab was an unheated, no electricity, no running water shed in the back yard, attached to the garage. School chums, members of a loosely organized "science club," helped me maintain it. Our equipment was pretty crude. We had no rubber stoppers; we used corks, in which we bored holes for glass tubing with a red-hot icepick, which we heated on the gas range in the kitchen. We used clothespins for test tube holders. We had no Bunsen burners, just alcohol lamps, which we made ourselves. We used 1.5 volt dry cells for electrolysis and silver and copper plating, and the cells had to last a long time, because they cost twenty-five cents (at Kress's). We got the silver by dissolving dimes in nitric acid.

My lab was actually not much different from the starting labs of most of the great chemists of history. Perhaps there was no absolute requirement that a future chemical genius start out with the most rudimentary lab possible, but it seems to have helped.

Joseph Priestley worked in his wife's kitchen. Charles Darwin had a lab in the gardener's shack. Tom Edison built his lab in his mother's basement; as did the young Linus Pauling. In Paris Louis Pasteur had two tiny rooms. The incubator was under the stairs, and could be entered only on hands and knees. The great German doctor, Robert Koch, discovered the tuberculosis bacillus in an eight-by-ten room at the back of his house, furnished by a bench and a stool. Paul Ehrlich (the first effective drug for syphilis – 606) got his personal lab in 1896 – two rooms. One was a former bakery, the other a former stable.

My prime example: Humphry Davy carried a small portable chest with chemical apparatus with him when he toured France in 1813. With this miniscule "lab" he isolated, identified, and named iodine as a new element.

The moral: you can do remarkable things though you have but a very crude and rudimentary lab. As I intended now to demonstrate.

I took a quarter spoonful of my wonderful new quick-acting gunpowder. Just to be safe I deposited it on the lab table a good four feet from the black mountain comprising the parent pile.

I lit the little sample with a match. I got an immediate beautiful violet fire. Several very hot molten globules spewed out. All but one dropped safely beside the burning sample. The one that didn't – exuberant, exultant – went the distance. It landed four feet away, on the summit of the mother cone. Events proceeded quickly. I ran to the door and stood there, holding it open, then I looked back, awed.

The cone turned into a blazing violet hemisphere. It didn't do it all at once. It needed several seconds to reach maximum brilliance and to begin its transformation into a humongous smoke cloud, which *pushed* me out of the door and then began its slow majestic ascent. As it rose it assumed the shape of a giant mushroom. I watched it go, up, up . . . I knew fire engines would be clanging our way any minute. I would be arrested, maybe sent to reform school (as had often been threatened for lesser crimes). The great cloud slowly drifted up and away, and eventually vanished over the horizon, headed for Dallas. The minutes passed. Nothing. I finally went back into my lab. The smoke was nearly gone. Nothing was burning. No flame or glowing coals anywhere. Just a big black charred circle on my lab table. Later, during supper (breaded pork chops, corn on the cob) Mother remarked that she wished the neighbors wouldn't burn trash in their backyards. I had made gunpowder. What was next? Nitroglycerine, of course. And again the question, how to make it. Irene Scather and I were not done.

I was thirteen when I found the Library Reference Room. I assumed I wasn't supposed to be there. The way Miss Scather ran the library, if something wasn't expressly permitted, it was safe to assume it was forbidden. This particular door was always closed. It *looked* off-limits. I checked for Miss Scather, then walked in and looked around. Inside were all sorts of fascinating things: a five-volume Oxford English Dictionary, a multivolume biographical encyclopedia, and about twenty volumes of Texas history.

To a Texan, history (meaning Texas history) is 90% of life. They teach it in grade school – the coming of the Austins, the wave of immigrants into Mexican Texas, the treacherous Mexicans, the Alamo (Thermopylae Had Its Messenger of Defeat; the Alamo Had None).

If Texas had anything, it had history, going way back. First, La Salle killed a suitable number of Indians and claimed it for the French. Then Spain stole it from the French. Then 130 years later, Mexico took it from Spain. In 1836 we gringoes stole it fair and square from the Mexicans, set up our Lone Star Republic, and we've been there ever since. In 1845 we got more or less annexed into the U.S., and then in 1861 into the Confederacy. (A real bummer.) So all in all, we had six flags.

But back to the Reference Room.

Next to the stately multi-volume Oxford English Dictionary were several oversized reference books dealing with cats, including a couple in foreign languages. Miss Scather was rumored to be a cat fancier. (Me, I preferred dogs.) I remember a picture of her in the *Star-Telegram* holding a cat cupped in one arm like a baby, while the other hand held some sort of trophy.

They also had the great *Encylopedia Britannica*. Within minutes after finding the "N" volume and the article on nitroglycerine, I felt a sharp pain in my right ear. I hadn't heard her come in. This was awful. I knew I was about to get evicted and my card cancelled. This was how Louis the XVI felt on the scaffold. I tried to shrink into my chair, I couldn't. The pain in my ear was too great. I heard a "crackle." She had crushed some of the cartilage.

"Well," rumbled Miss Scather (she was tall and solid, and she had a heavy voice, probably like that of George Jeffries, Charles II's hanging judge), "it's refreshing to see young minds engaged in real research, but I believe we should begin at the proper level. Come." With thumb and forefinger she pulled me up.

"Ow," I said softly. She took no notice. We walked lock-step out of the Reference Room and on toward the stairs leading to the upstairs juvenile section.

Now, under the stairwell is a life-size artifact, a mannequin representing a Chinaman pulling a rickshaw. God alone knows how it got there. The eyes are very realistic, and now they looked at me, and the corners wrinkled in subtle mockery.

That wasn't the worst. Just then a girl in pigtails was coming in from the street. She fixed jeering caught-you-didn't-she eyes on me. I knew her. Helen Dyess. She ran up the stairs, looked back briefly, then disappeared into the children's room.

The Guardian of the Books released my ear, and I proceeded upward on my own.

Scather had been too late. In those last precious seconds in the Reference Room I had memorized how to make nitroglycerine. You simply pour glycerine slowly into a chilled mixture of nitric and sulfuric acids.

A few days later, back in my lab, I carried out the reaction in an old ink bottle. With great care I placed the bottle on top of the back fence facing the alley. I got my air rifle. I sat on the steps of the back porch, some fifteen yards away. I took aim. Just then the earth began to vibrate. The mule-drawn garbage wagon was coming down the alley. The back fence trembled. I watched in awe and horror. The ink bottle fell over into the alley, in front of the mule. I ducked and put my hands over my eyes.

And . . . nothing.

No astonished mule rising into the sky. No atomized garbage man or garbage.

Subsequent nervous investigation showed that the bottle had landed exactly upside down, and that everything had run out into the ground.

Well, okay. Maybe for the time being I should forget nitroglycerine. Plain gunpowder seemed safer, more predictable.

I made some more gunpowder.

Yes, chemists love explosions. If they say they don't, they lie. Explosions are blazing audible proof of the interreactivity of the elements – and *that* is the whole foundation, the entire encapsulated truth of the science of chemistry.

And to achieve a fine explosion they didn't mind risking life and limb.

They all loved getting blown up with fulminates. Why all the interest in fulminates? Well, for one thing, fulminates were easy to make. Dissolve silver in nitric acid, add ethanol, you get a precipitate of silver fulminate. The fun begins when you recover and dry the product. Tickling dry fulminate with a feather can set it off.

Justus von Liebig, the famous German chemist, almost lost his eyesight when fulminic acid exploded under his nose. Jöns Berzelius, the great Swedish analytical chemist, was almost killed in an explosion of gold fulminate.

Humphry Davy, the famous English chemist and inventor of the miner's safety lamp, got careless with nitrogen trichloride, the most attractive exploder after the fulminates. The flask exploded and injured his eyes. He needed help, so he hired young Michael Faraday as his secretary. To show his appreciation, the first thing Faraday did was to knock himself unconscious with an exploding flask of nitrogen trichloride. Juvenile gunpowder makers had a better survival record.

Tom Edison went through his gunpowder phase, of course, but he took it a step further than most boys. He made a cannon out of a hollow log, loaded it with several pounds of gunpowder of his own design, and proceeded to demolish the local ice-house. As a boy Linus Pauling, the great American scientist, made gunpowder and put it on the streetcar tracks. (So did I.)

Sometimes these little explosions have surprising consequences. Thus:

Mother's bedroom faced the backyard and her Westinghouse sewing machine sat near the back window, where there was plenty of light. She was sitting there, sewing ten sets of angel wings for the Sunday School play, coming up Sunday, tomorrow. Sewing these things was a slow ticklish business, and she was not doing well. Tunney's incessant barking was making her nervous, and she was making mistakes.

Tunney was our collie dog. The name was a misnomer, for she was a female. Tunney was barking at Pa Ferguson, who was a big long-haired black cat, unneutered and unamiable. Pa Ferguson (of unknown origin and ownership – we named him after the impeached Texas governor) loved to sit on our back fence, just out of reach, and sneer and leer down at our fearless infuriated defender of the turf. For variety Pa would walk with unhurried mincing steps the length of the fence, then back again, with Tunney exactly under him, every inch, hoping, hoping.

Mother called out to me to please take the dog for a walk, and this I did. When I came back, the cat was gone, and I returned Tunney to the back yard. But our troubles were not over because meanwhile the ice-box had overflowed.

In the mid-twenties the ice-box was just that – a big box with a big chamber to hold a 50 or 75 or 100-pound cake of ice with compartments and trays and bins. You couldn't freeze anything in it, but it preserved things pretty well. The problem was the big cake of ice. The ice melted, and the melt water had to go somewhere. Customarily, a hole was drilled in the floor under the ice-box (back porch, cupboard, kitchen, wherever – ours was in the kitchen), and a one-inch drain pipe was stuck down in the hole and then led at a 90-degree turn straight out in the crawl space under the house to a spot in the back yard that could absorb the slow drip. It all worked fine, except every few months the drain pipe would plug with algae. Slimy stuff. When you saw the puddle under the ice-box, you knew it was time to blow out the drain pipe.

It was my job to blow, and I hated it. I had to get down on my hands and knees outside in the mud, take the wet cruddy pipe end in my mouth, make a face, then blast away with all possible lung power. The stuff always tasted awful. I could taste it for a long time afterwards.

No. This time, I was going to blow the pipe scientifically.

First making sure Mother was busy at her sewing machine, I went out to my lab, got my equipment, and then returned to the kitchen.

Now, the ice-box was on rollers. I rolled it out a couple of feet, put a shallow pan under it to catch the drip temporarily, and mopped up the puddle around the drain pipe. I swabbed out the top two inches of the pipe (which was as far down as I could reach). It still looked wet. I poured a little alcohol into the pipe and lit it with a kitchen match. That dried things out pretty well. Next, I stuffed in a little cotton swabbing and tamped it down. Then my prize steelie, actually not a real marble, but a half-inch ball bearing, and a winner in neighborhood marble matches. And then more cotton wadding, followed by a spoonful of my choicest gunpower.

Abe Lincoln hadn't permitted potassium chlorate in Federal gun barrels because it scoured the internals. I was using it because it would do exactly that: scour the internals of this accursed drain pipe.

My fuse assembly was pretty neat – a cork with a quarter-inch hole down the center. I pushed the cork down the drain pipe until it rested on the gunpowder. Then I filled the fuse hole with gunpowder. I listened. I couldn't risk any interruptions by Mother. I could hear the faint hum of the Westinghouse. Okay. I started to strike the match, but then I stopped. Tunney was barking again. And the Westinghouse had stopped. Was Mother about to come into the kitchen? Oh boy! I had to head her off. I ran around to the bedroom. She was still there, sitting at her machine, and talking to someone, in a casual conversational voice, with the same intonation she'd use with me or Peedo, like explaining why we had to eat our carrots or why we had to take a bath, something like that. Reasonable but firm. Except there was nobody there. She said: "God, those animals are driving me crazy. If that dog doesn't stop barking, You won't have any angels tomorrow. It's up to You."

I raced back to the kitchen. I struck the match. I held the flame to the little pinch of powder on top of the cork. It flared up instantly. The burning powder sizzled down the hole in the cork. The charge in the pipe caught.

And then various things happened all at once. There was a heck of a bang. The kitchen floor shook. There was a moment's stunning silence, and then Tunney's barks suddenly tripled in fury and volume. I rushed to the back door. She was chasing Pa Ferguson in narrow circles all around the yard. He was yowling and spitting and he looked – *different.* But he finally got his bearings, headed for the fence, and with a magnificent leap worthy of a jaguar, sailed over it with a foot to spare and disappeared down into the alley.

Tunney of course fussed around importantly for a little while, yelling things like, "Come back and fight, you scummy coward!" But when she was convinced the ancient enemy was gone, she trotted back to me. "I did good, didn't I, Bubba?" "You sure did." We opened the gate and went out into the alley together, just to look around. Tunney found it right away – a furry black strip, about 7 or 8 inches long, bloody at one end. I had shot off Pa Ferguson's tail. I left it there. Tunney scratched dirt over it with her back paws, and while she was busy with this I retrieved my steelie, which was shining in the middle of the alley. It had one little blood stain, which I wiped off on my pants. We went back in. I had to clean up in the kitchen before anybody started asking questions.

From then on everything worked. Mother finished the angel wings all in good time. I pulled the cork and pushed the ice-box back over the drain, which soon began dripping obediently.

In fact, during my remaining years in Fort West, it never again stopped up. Mother knew something was not quite right, but she figured God had taken care of everything in His own way, and that it would be discourteous to ask questions.

We never saw Pa Ferguson again.

A week later there was this odd item in the *Star-Telegram*. Miss Irene Scather, organizer of the Annual Fort West Cat Show, had withdrawn her entrant, the famous Champion Attila, a black long-hair Persian, because of a serious injury involving his tail.

Scary.

I later learned (to my great chagrin) that she had taken to her bed for three days. Chagrin, yes, because had I known it at the time, this would have meant a three-day pass to every nook and cranny in the Library.

Yes, Miss Scather and I went way back.

So it was indeed the ogress here in Chief Goodall's office, apparently now retired from the book shelves, but still actively protecting Texas minds.

She was just as I recalled her, heavy, angular, grimly corsetted. Her mouth still had that downward set, as though the result of facial surgery, and her cheeks were still drawn into hard vertical lines.

Chief Goodall continued, "Miss Scather is collecting information concerning certain teachers in the public schools. The League will make this information available to prospective employers of these persons."

This was the famous League Blacklist. I had heard of it.

He continued in a glum monotone, "Miss Scather has asked us to search our records for a Miss . . ." He adjusted his spectacles and squinted at a piece of paper. "Sybyl . . . ?"

He looked over his glasses at his visitor.

"*Cybele,* Chief Goodall." She spelled it out in a dry broken hiss. "C-Y-B-E-L-E. Cybele Wilson."

I stopped breathing.

"Ah, yes. Unusual first name." He handed me the slip. "Take a look, will you, Barnes. Shouldn't take long. We'll wait."

"Yes, sir." It was sort of a two-syllable gulp. I turned to go.

"Not so fast, young man," she said sternly. "I'll go with you."

She must have sensed there was something about me she couldn't trust. In this, she was quite right. On the other hand, the files were off limits to the public.

I looked back at the chief. He rolled his eyes, then nodded.

Whoa! *Indeed not so fast!* Did Cybele in fact have a record? Suppose she had been visiting her mother when vice raided the Big House? They would have hauled her in along with the regular girls. There would be a record. Would it matter, now that she was dying? Of course it would! More than ever! Oh, *damn* you, Scather!

I said quickly, "Chief, I had to leave a couple of s.c.'s with the turnkey. Take just a moment to finish printing them."

"Sure. Get them out of there."

"'S.c.'s?' " said Miss Scather.

"Suspicious characters," he explained as I hurried out.

Back in the record room I got to work. First I checked the three-by-five arrest cards. Sure enough. Cybele Wilson, June 9, 1925, Vice Squad, E. Second Street. It gave the fingerprint class. I looked around, nobody near. I snapped the three-by-five out of the file and stuck it in my pocket. Next, the fingerprint card. I had to fold it a couple of times, and then into my pocket. Her only remaining police record would be the blotter – one sheet now stored under ten big heavy 365-page volumes and moldering away in the sub-basement. Let it lie.

The entire felonious destruction of records had taken only seconds.

So now, back in the chief's office. "Follow me, please," I told her.

I led her back into the record room. "If she's here, we'll have her in two places: in the three-by-five arrest cards, filed alphabetically, and in the fingerprint cards, filed by fingerprint classification. We'll check the arrest cards first."

Very slowly, we flipped the little cards: Wilkins, Williams, Willis, Wilner, Wilson. Dozens of Wilsons. But no Cybele. Or Sybyl. We checked them again. I got the file drawer out and laid it on the table, and she checked the cards herself.

Again, no Cybele.

I looked up thoughtfully at this Defender of the Faith. "Maybe she didn't give her right name?"

Miss Scather took a wheezy breath. I could hear her corset stays squeaking and shifting. Finally everything seemed to reach a strained equilibrium. "Couldn't say."

"On the other hand," I said, "even if she used an alias, we'd still have her in the fingerprints. But to find her fingerprint card, we'd have to have her fingerprint classification. Let's see now. Was she ever in the Texas school system?"

"Yes, as a matter of fact, she was. She taught at JimBowie High."

I looked thoughtful. "I think I'd better call the State School Registrar, in Austin, get her fingerprint class. Take just a moment. Can you wait?"

"Of course."

This was horrid mockery. I should hate myself, but I didn't. It was this, or strangle her. I felt like that character in Poe's "The Cask of Amontillado," howling in jeering unison with his imprisoned enemy.

I put the call through. While we were waiting, I asked Miss Scather, "What did she teach?"

"Something . . . quite horrid . . . chemistry, I think."

"Chemistry? Oh dear. Sounds serious." I grimaced. "Isn't that sort of like the anarchists? Explosions? Bad smells?"

"Oh, much worse, young man. Godless creatures . . . atheists . . . evolutionists!" She separated the words like cannon firing in sequence. "Degenerates, all, with diseased minds."

I gave a low whistle. "Oh, this is terrible! I can see our job is cut out for us. We have to protect society from these people."

She ground it out. "Especially young minds."

"Especially."

The phone rang. It was Austin calling back. The ex-librarian breathed heavily over my shoulder as I wrote down the classification. She followed me lock-step as I pulled out the proper print drawer and flipped through the cards. I pointed and shrugged. "That's where it would be if we had her."

"Maybe it was misfiled?"

"Not likely. Every card that is filed carries a red clip. The clip alerts another clerk to double check whether it is correctly filed. He checks, then pulls the clip." I shook my head. "Quite odd, but it looks like we don't have any record of her."

She thanked me profusely. "It's a great comfort and pleasure to meet a person with genuine civic pride. With young men like you, Texas is in good hands."

I quite agreed. I bowed deeply. "Thank you, Miss Scather, it was a pleasure to work with you on this. It's been a real education."

As she walked away I thought of Cybele, stretched out to die in the Big House. My heartbeat had slowed to normal but the adrenalin still flowed and my ear still tingled. I had to do something.

Having destroyed, it was only fair to create. I sat down at my typewriter and typed up an authentic-looking arrest card.

Scather, Irene
15 April 1920, Soliciting lower Commerce.
4 Sept 1923, Bootlegging. Referred to Feds.
10 May 1923, Operating male brothel in basement Public Library.
1 June 1924, Failure to report for Wasserman.

I filed it and instantly felt a lot better. My ear slowly untingled.

She wrote Chief Goodall a nice letter about the service his Department had provided, and noted particularly "that nice young Mr. Burns." I'm told the Chief just shook his head and stuck it in my personnel file.

I saw Cybele every day as she lay dying. They put her in Di's upstairs room, the one with the air conditioner. Toward the end I simply moved in with her. Di gave me a cot by the window.

When Mother got the facts she tried hard to decide whether to be horrified. Poor Mom. She discussed it with the minister, she prayed over it, and finally she gave up. No decision. It was beyond comprehension.

Peedo was philosophical. I had never made much sense to him anyhow.

Every night, during those last few weeks, I asked her to marry me. She always refused. At least it made her laugh, and that was good. But I was serious. Why would I want to marry a dying woman? Because she was Cybele, and we loved greatly. I got a marriage license form at the courthouse and thumbtacked it on the wall by her telephone. All it needed was a few signatures and registration in the courthouse. But no.

Ashes

People came to see her. She still had a few friends from JimBowie High, and there were doctors, a minister or two. She made her will via Di's lawyer. Nobody seemed to mind that she had chosen this part of town to die in. The girls up and down the street followed her condition closely.

The whole Police Department knew what was going on with me and Cybele. They didn't really understand, but at least they were sympathetic. They talked about us in little groups, and they'd fall silent as I passed. For the time being the vice squad canceled all raids on East Second Street.

She became incontinent and wore a diaper. Di cared for her as though she were a three-month infant.

I have been in sickrooms before. Each has its own distinctive odor. Her room was different. There were plenty of flowers, of course. Bouquets, sprays, in vases, on tables, and so on. But all that was background. What you smelled, the odor that hit you, was bluebonnets. But there weren't any. The scent was coming from her.

Every afternoon when I left for work, I kissed her goodbye, and wondered if it were the last time. She had long ago stopped dying by inches. Now it was by feet, yards, miles. She and grinning Death were racing hand in bony hand down to the finish line.

On that last day I started to call in, take a day of leave, but she insisted I go on, she'd be fine. I thought about it. To stay would mean I thought she was going to die within hours.

So I went on.

Late that evening Di called me back.

As I came into the room and saw my darling, I thought she was already dead. Even within those few intervening hours, she had changed. Her white translucent skin was stretched tight over her cheeks. The sheet was partially drawn back, and her ribs were visible through her nightgown. The sheet covered one hand. The other lay on it like a white claw. Her eyes were bright, brilliant.

She saw me and whispered something. I came over and knelt, with my ear close to her lips.

She whispered again. *"Jesu . . ."*

I got up, located the new electric phonograph, then the record of the great Bach chorale. I put the needle into the starting groove, turned the volume low, and returned to her. I held her hand. It was icy, and growing even colder, if that were possible. Save for the Bach, there was silence. Then the music came to an end and the machine shut itself off.

We waited.

She was whispering again. "Don't leave me . . ."

"No . . . I will not leave you." I wasn't really talking. I was gasping and gurgling. "We will be together . . . always."

Her eyes opened wide. She looked at me. *Through* me. Through the walls, at something far, far ahead. Her lips wrinkled into her characteristic gay grin. She was seeing something invisible to the rest of us, and it was making her very happy. She whispered, "Our child, Joe . . . so beautiful . . . she . . ."

Then there was a horrid rattle in her throat, and she was dead.

Sad, sad that at the very last, she was hallucinating. We had no child. We could never have a child.

I bent over her. I kissed lips that were not lips. I kissed the shrunken neck. I dropped hot tears on her chest. My arms were under her. I was clutching and hugging her and kissing her and running my mouth over the thing that passed for her body. I pulled her shoulder straps down and in a well-remembered ritual I kissed pink spots that had once been breasts. It was a holy rite, it was sacred, and maybe a little obscene. I was wild.

Di grabbed me and pulled me back to reality. She brought over a basin of warm water, washrags, towels. "She soiled herself. I'll have to wash her."

"No. I'll do it. She's my wife." It would be the closest I would get to changing a diaper on our baby. They yielded.

With two fingers joined in gentle benediction I pulled the eyelids down. We noted then that her withered right hand clutched a small New Testament, and the little book held a dried fragile spray stalk of barely recognizable bluebonnet. When I took the little volume it fell open automatically at the flower marker, and I read the underlined passage. I closed the book and put it in my pocket. Di alone seemed to notice. She did not object.

And so I washed and dried and powdered the organic machine that had once sheltered her soul. Then I stood back with the others. We looked at the face. It shone.

This was awesome. We all knew we had witnessed a tremendous thing. Whatever it was, this was not a death.

After that, we opened the special box containing her final attire. There was a wonderful odor: a whole field of bluebonnets. And so we dressed her in the long pink nightgown with a lacey night jacket, all decorated in tiny bluebonnets.

The rest was anticlimactic formality. Services at St. Joseph's Sanctuary, in the Cup Chapel. All the girls came, of course. Di rented a somber black suit for Mr. Sandt. Miss Meigs, the JimBowie librarian, attended, and several of Cybele's students from past years; but no teachers. Mr. Feingarten was there. He sat next to the girls. He and I exchanged brief glances. He just shook his head. Odd, I noted he didn't wipe his glasses. For this occasion of state he must have shampooed his eyebrows. Perhaps for the first time ever. It was said that Mr. Vachel, the principal, had had to make a sudden trip to Lubbock to visit an ailing aunt.

It was a closed-coffin service. She was to be cremated. Father Paul, the Sanctuary prior, gave a brief elegy. It seems he taught her chemistry when she attended school there. The choir sang the *Jesu.*

I have mentioned the Cup Chapel, the little brick building where they kept an allegedly remarkable Cup. The people who ran the Sanctuary believed it was the very cup Jesus had drunk from, at the Last Supper. In funerals, it was customary for one of the brothers of the Order to bring the Cup over and place it on the coffin, so that the soul would receive the blessing of the Cup.

I watched the cassocked cup carrier as he performed his office. There was something about him. Did I know him? Yes. Despite the hidden face, hands concealed by long drooping sleeves, I knew him. And he knew me. Lukey Gruen turned his face toward me briefly, nodded, placed the Cup reverently, turned, walked back to his position off to the side of the chamber.

Lukey, I thought, for God's sake . . . Well, to each his own. But *this?*

And so the Cup sat for its appointed hour on her coffin.

So this was *the* Cup – with a capital C. The mysterious cup in the painting. All silly superstition, of course, but there it was – an inert siliceous artifact that wielded power because superstitious self-deluding minds believed in it. What did they think it was going to do? Bust out with a miracle before their credulous hopeful eyes? For better or worse, it just sat there, and nothing at all happened.

There was some talk about an insurance policy, but aside from that she died nearly broke. Di paid the last debts to the hospital. Cybele left me all her books. Chemistry, physics . . . science . . . several on gardening. And fiction . . . some classics, like *Lorna Doone,* but a lot of junk, too. Plus a few things that could have got her in serious trouble with the school board: Stowe's *Uncle Tom's Cabin, Three Weeks,* by Elinor Glynn, Flaubert's *Madame Bovary.* I wasn't surprised.

The day after the cremation Di and I drove out into the country with the urn containing the ashes.

We talked. It was a brooding, broken, intermittent conversation.

I said, "I never understood what she saw in me."

"She was able to talk to you. You were the only one, ever. Not even Father Paul . . . "

I didn't say anything.

She continued, "She was a virgin, you know. You were her first . . . and only."

"Yes.

"She wants you to get married."

"I'm already married . . . to her."

"You know what I mean . . . what she meant."

"Yes. Someday, maybe."

"Joe, she wants you to get back into chemistry. She left a little insurance money for you. She asked SCU to send your transcript to George Washington University, in Washington, D.C. They have a first-class science night school. She got her degrees in chemistry there. I know you have to work. Your family needs the money. You could go to school at night and work for the government in the day, send money home."

"I'll think about it."

We turned off into a side road. I pulled over onto the shoulder and stopped the car. It was the right place. We got out and looked around.

We stood in a sea of bluebonnets. *Lupinus subcarnosus,* Texas state flower, about a foot tall. The blossoms resemble tiny blue bonnets, like those worn by pioneer women. We floated in fragrance.

Now, it was a beautiful sunny day in mid-May. It had rained the day before, but the air was now bright and clear.

We walked out into the field. We didn't shed a tear. The ashes . . . I scattered some, she scattered some. It was over quickly. There wasn't much to scatter. Amazing how a human being can boil down to nearly nothing.

The Big House re-opened for business as usual. I moved my meager belongings back into my room in Mother's house. To the great relief of all.

The vice squad phoned Di to set up a mutually acceptable date for a raid.

And life goes on. It goes, but it doesn't go anywhere. We begin, and end, in the middle.

The Cup

The burglary report started at the top. At 4 a.m. Father Paul, the Prior of St. Joseph's Sanctuary, phoned Police Chief Stahl, who finally understood that *the* Cup had been stolen, and promised to send out two of his top detectives at once. Plus me, as the only fingerprint man available.

In huffy silence, at 5 a.m. Schultz, Ebbitts, and I drove out together in Schultz's car to the Sanctuary on Camp Bowie. I was sleepy but curious. This was the place of Cybele's funeral, and long before, she had gone to school here. Mrs. Gaither had painted that mysterious portrait, where she was holding a replicant of this very cup. Already I was having confused feelings about the investigation.

Schultz's feelings were not confused. They were pure, crystalline: he muttered, "Got out of bed for a damn cup."

A damn cup? Schultzie, I thought, you're in for a surprise.

In the dim morning light we could see that the buildings of the priory were surrounded by fields of bluebonnets, waving and rippling. I could smell them. My heart began to pound. I thought of her.

We were met at the gate by a monk clad in a long gray cloak roped about the waist, and sandals. He could have walked out of a thirteenth century Franciscan monastery. I said, "Hello, Lukey. Good to see you."

Holding a cane with his left hand he pulled back the long right sleeve of his cloak and we shook hands. I noticed that his right wrist was bandaged. "Joseph." He grinned. "Officially I'm Brother Lucas."

I introduced him to my two companions. He got in the back seat of the car with me and gave Schultz directions to a building in the center of the complex. I knew with grim foreboding which building: it would be the Cup Chapel, where Father Paul had preached his short sermon over her closed coffin. On that simple wooden box the Cup had stood on its silver platter.

There was unfinished business here, and Fate had decreed my return. Schultz asked questions on the way. "This cup, how much is it insured for?"

Luke said, "Thirty thousand dollars, I'm told. Actually, though, it is priceless."

"Yeah? An heirloom?"

"In a sense."

"You have photographs, of course," Schultz said.

"As a matter of fact –" Brother Lucas reached into the recesses of his robes and pulled out a five-by-seven glossy, which he handed up to Ebbitts. "As you can see, it's just a plain glass cup, about three-quarters pint. Clear glass, rather thick. No handles. Tapered. About four inches in diameter at the rim, three inches at the bottom, about four inches high."

Schultz glanced at the photo and grunted, "Doesn't look like much."

"No, it doesn't," agreed Brother Lucas.

"My wife bought a set just like that at Woolworth's," offered Ebbitts.

Brother Lucas smiled faintly.

We parked near the chapel and followed Luke inside. He limped, but shuffled along at a goodly pace. By the dim lights we could see a small stand on the altar, covered in black velvet, and in the center, a silver plate, empty.

"It just sat there?" asked Schultz glumly. "On that plate? People come and go, anybody can pick up something worth thirty grand?"

"It was very holy," Luke said. "We didn't think anyone would touch it. We have always considered it to be quite safe."

"Safe?" said Schultz. "How's that?"

I was working on the plate, dusting it with MgO. Nothing stuck. Now was a good time to keep my mouth shut. I didn't. "Some say that this is the Holy Grail – the cup that Jesus drank from, and passed around to his disciples, at the Last Supper."

Schultz was about to get his notebook out and take some notes, but that stopped him. He turned, looked at me strangely, then back to Brother Lucas.

"That right?"

"Yes," Luke said gravely.

"Jesus!" whispered Ebbitts.

"Exactly," said Brother Lucas.

Schultz sighed and put his notebook away. "You get any prints?" he asked me.

"No, the platter was wiped clean, and of course the velvet won't show anything."

"Funny, they didn't take the platter," Schultz said thoughtfully.

I was thinking approximately the same thing. Also the absence of prints was trying to tell me something.

"Might as well look around," Schultz said. He nodded to Ebbitts, who then stayed behind to check the chapel interior more thoroughly.

Luke showed us a couple of adjoining storage rooms, then we went out onto a screened porch in the back.

I sniffed. "Cleaning fluid?"

Luke pointed to an open pot on a table in the corner. "The janitor is working on the drapes."

I noted a jug under the table, labeled Benzene. And another, Carbon Tetrachloride. Curious.

Ebbitts rejoined us. "Well," Schultz said, "that about it? Okay, we might as well get back. Mr. Gruen, if you get any ransom calls, stall him, let me know right away. Here's my card, with my number."

"Of course."

"Meanwhile we'll monitor the local pawnshops, but I've got to warn you, and meaning no disrespect, there's not a pawnshop in the state of Texas that'd give you a nickel for that cup."

"You're probably right," said the cloaked man.

We walked back through the chapel and out to the car.

Luke asked me, "Joe, can you stay a while? I'll drive you back."

"Sure."

He and I stood there on the chapel steps and watched the car pull away.

"They don't believe," he mused.

"I don't believe it's genuine either, Luke."

"I know. But at least you admit the possibility."

"A remote possibility. Face it, Luke, two thousand years is a bit much."

He laughed. "There are pieces much older in the British Museum. Joe, you're hopeless. Let's go over to my office. I'll give you a cup of coffee."

We sat in hard-backed chairs near the window. He took a sip and grimaced.

I blurted, "What's with the bandages, Luke? The cane? What happened?"

He seemed to study me, but couldn't come to a decision. "You want the plausible or the implausible?"

"Start with the plausible.

"Well, you remember those phosphorus splatters . . ."

"You still have lesions? After all this time? Come on, Lukey!"

"Joe," he said carefully, "okay, it's not really phosphorus lesions. I thought it was, at first, but it isn't. It's the stigmata – the wounds of our Lord on the cross." He was dead serious.

My face went blank. I didn't know what to say.

He said, "I know it's hard to accept. I didn't believe it at first myself."

I found my voice. "Listen, Lukey, you should go back on medication. It can't be the *real* stigmata. You'd also have lashes on your back, wounds on your feet . . ." I looked at his cane. My voice trailed off.

He laughed softly. "Plus a hole in the gut, where the spear went in."

I was in over my head. I closed my eyes and made a low gurgling sound. "Why, Lukey? What for?"

"Not sure. May have something to do with *you.* "

"Me? How so?"

"It came on me during her funeral, when I was carrying the Cup to her coffin. I think she wants me to help you."

"Funny way to tell you."

"No . . . you have to understand these things . . . something to do with the Cup, of course."

The Cup. Well, why not? "Tell me about the Cup."

He smiled. "I promise I won't try to convince you of anything. I know better. Still, you might be interested in the traditions. Okay?"

"Of course."

"In the first place, there are three Josephs in the Bible, all good guys, all saints: Joseph the father of Jesus; Joseph, son of Jacob; and Joseph of Arimathea, who gave his tomb to Jesus. St. Joseph's Sanctuary is *that* St. Joseph. Okay?"

"So far."

He continued. "Facts: there was a Cup. Jesus drank from it at The Last Supper."

"No argument," I said.

"Now begins tradition. From here on in, the Cup and Joseph of Arimathea are inseparable." He took another sip and looked out the window. "You won't find the village of Arimathea on any modern map. Today it is dust and ruins. In Biblical times, though, it was a thriving little village about twenty miles northwest of Jerusalem. Our Joseph was born there, but probably lived most of his life in Jerusalem, where he could watch over his numerous enterprises. For he was a rich man, a pillar of the Jewish community and an active member of the Sanhedrin. He owned shops, ships, mines, vineyards, olive groves. His factories made glassware, metal goods, dyes, perfumes. Subsequent events suggest that he had profitable commercial contacts throughout the Roman world, including Caesarea, Puteoli, Rome, Alexandria, and north into Britain."

He studied me across the table. "Am I boring you?"

"I'll let you know." I must have had a vacant look on my face. Actually, I was thinking more about that cleaning fluid on the back porch than about Joseph of Arimathea. Dangerous stuff.

"All right then," he said. "Back to that crucial Passover in Jerusalem. Probably our Joseph owned the house where Jesus celebrated the Passover supper with his disciples, and by prior arrangement Peter and John met his servant – identified by the water jar – who led them to the house. The upper room was already furnished with table and benches, together with dishes, bowls, plates, cups. Their host would send up food and drink at the proper time. The tableware was undoubtedly common everyday items, probably made in local shops, quite possibly in Joseph's own factories. It is unlikely that any one of the wine cups was significantly different from any of the others.

"Now, according to tradition Joseph's housekeeper cleaned up the room the next day, and on Joseph's instruction, he or she salvaged Jesus's cup as a souvenir, identified probably by servants and maids who had served the group the previous evening.

"So the Cup went into the reverent and permanent possession of our Arimathean. And next we have the sudden growth of the first Christian congregations and their attempted slaughter by Nero in 37 A.D., whereupon Joseph took the Cup and fled to England, where he built the first English church at Glastonbury, in Somerset. The building has long since disappeared, and in fact the abbey built over the ruins in the twelfth century itself now lies in ruins, the result of deliberate destruction by minions of the eighth Henry.

"A lone tower, built onto a fragment of the original structures, stands like a brave beacon on the hilltop. Sheep graze safely on the hillside. Bach would have approved. There's a roadway straight up to the tower, and a circling footpath on the other side. Otherwise the only functioning memento of Joseph is the so-called Glastonbury thorn, a bushy variety flowering at Christmas, which according to tradition grew from Joseph's staff when he stuck it in the ground and announced that there he would build his church, the first Christian church in England. Cromwell thought the thorn bushes were all papish superstition, and his Roundheads chopped them down. But a sprig or two escaped, and flourished. Joseph's original, of course, was thought by many to have come from Jesus's Crown of Thorns.

"Well, back to Joseph. In 72 A.D. he died, and the Cup passed to his son, and when *he* died, to *his* son, and so on down the line."

"To the present day?" I said.

Luke smiled. "Well, perhaps only by courtesy of title. I doubt that the present Keeper, our good Father Paul, is a lineal descendant of the original Joseph. But some of the earlier guardians apparently carried the blood but without the nobility of soul. Indeed, some of the early custodians were all too human. Their frailties were grists to the mills of medieval minstrels. You probably know the legends. The Cup moves to the Continent. King Amfortas, grandson of Joseph, sinned with a pagan lady, and fought a heathen knight, whose lance wounded him in his genitals and made him impotent. It was torture, and he wanted to die, but the Grail kept him alive. The kingdom became a desolate wasteland. He could not ride, or stand. Prone, he could fish. The minstrels sang about him. He was the Fisher King. He would be healed only when a saintly knight asked him the right question. In the British version, it was Galahad; in the German, it was Parzival. In other versions these two goodly champions are close friends; in still others they merge into one. It doesn't matter, except insofar as it bears on custody of the Cup. Nor does the Question matter. The only thing of importance to us is that the Cup has come down to us for safekeeping, and now it is missing."

I looked away, up at the ceiling. I didn't want him to see that I didn't believe any of this. I was reminded that if all fragments of the True Cross were collected from reliquaries all over the world, the stack would top the Empire State Building. I said, "Any suspects?"

He sighed. "The janitor, perhaps."

"The man who was cleaning the drapes?"

"Him."

I thought about the cleaning fluid. There was something there, but I couldn't quite grab it. I temporized. "Just my own curiosity, why do they call it the 'grail'?"

"That one's easy. 'Grail' is a corruption of 'Gradalis', Latin for cup."

I finished my coffee. Out of politeness. It was terrible. "Luke, you didn't really need me for this. And it doesn't make any difference whether I or Schultz or anybody believes your cup is the true and only Holy Grail. What's really on your mind? Why did you ask me to stay?"

He seemed mildly surprised that I had read him so easily. "You're right. It was Father Paul's idea. He has a message for you."

Curiouser and curiouser. "How did he know I was here?"

"I phoned him when you and the detectives were checking out the chapel."

"He wants to see me?"

"No. He said I could tell you."

"Shoot."

"There are three things. First, he quotes Father Jacques de Moulin, *Recherches sur le Sangreal* – 1546: 'The holy cup has a will of its own. It has the power of life and death, and it appears when and where it is needed.'" He watched my face. "Got that?"

"Yeah, I *guess* so." Should I be taking notes, I wondered. But what for? Nothing made any sense.

"Second," continued Luke, "he believes the Cup is somewhere in the chapel."

That was interesting. "Schultz and Ebbitts – the top eyes in the Bureau – missed it?"

"Maybe. Anyhow, could we go back, take one more look?"

I looked at his cane. "You're up to it?"

"Of course."

We returned. We spaced the interior in grids and searched it square by square. We looked under every pew, every chair.

We looked into every confessional. We looked overhead into the lights. We looked behind half a dozen plaster saints. We took our time. He paced along with his cane.

I knew it was futile. Schultz and Ebbitts had their faults, but with this kind of thing they were very good. And they hadn't found it. Of course, they didn't believe it was truly the Grail, but that wouldn't have made them any less thorough.

The invisible Holy Grail. I thought of H.G. Wells and his *Invisible Man*. They'd shown the movie at the Palace just a couple of years earlier. Claude Rains had achieved invisibility because his body had the same index of refraction as that of air. That made him transparent.

Luke and I walked on. We finished a side hall and a unisex washroom. He followed me out onto the back porch, which was screened to let in the breeze but keep out bugs. We checked it all again. On a bench was a confessional drape arranged to show a dark green spot. A sponge lay next to a glass measuring pitcher. The bucket of carbon tet was still there. I sniffed.

Luke walked over to the bench and looked at the vessel. "Inflammable?"

"Carbon tetrachloride isn't, but I think he's mixing it with benzene, which is." I stepped over and looked down into the clear liquid. Nothing there.

The robed man sighed. "I guess that's it. I'll drive you back to town."

As we drove in, I said, "You said the prior had three messages for me. What's number three?"

"He says you know where the Cup is."

It took a while for that to sink in, and then a while to get my heart started again. "You mean –"

"Oh, dear no. You didn't steal it, Joe. He knows that. But he thinks you know where it is . . . where the thief put it."

"He's crazy."

Luke made an odd lifting motion with his right shoulder. We were both silent the rest of the way in.

"Call me," he said.

I didn't reply. I was thinking, Lukey, why are you doing this to your body? Surely God – if there is a God – doesn't require it. It's all in your head. You're either very sick or very holy. Either way, you need a doctor. It is 1:30 in the afternoon. I am walking north on Commerce. I turn off on East Seventh, headed – where? I'm not certain. I'm thinking so hard I'm not sure where I am. I bump into people. I'm at the ticket window of the Palace. I show my badge. She shrugs, waves me on in.

I head for the balcony. It's dark, dark. I can't see very well. My eyes gradually adjust. I search out the top row, under the projector beam, where we used to sit. Anybody there? No?

Wait. That fragrance. Over and above the smell of stale air and rancid popcorn. Olfactory hallucination? I went on up and sat down. I sat there, silent, not moving, thinking of her. Our first time here. And then again. And again. Dark secret trysts. And now I sit on her right. I am leaning over toward her. My left hand holds the back of her head, my right slides up her inner thigh. Our lips lock. Her chest is moving, but she is silent because she is breathing into my mouth. Climax and desperate gasps. But this time, not the usual crowning collapse and silence. She is whispering. She is trying to tell me something.

She fades. No one is there, not anywhere near me. No more Cybele. No more bluebonnets.

I realize I have been watching an old rerun: *The Invisible Man.* Curious. Very curious. Because there it was: the solution. I knew. Maybe.

I had to get back to the Bureau. I had to telephone Luke, preferably with Schultz on the extension.

The Hearing

And now things moved smoothly. I went back to the office, found Schultz, and asked him to get on the other line while I talked to Luke on the phone. He did.

I told Luke where to find the Cup.

Later that afternoon Schultz complained to our mutual boss, Chief of Detectives Walter Goodall. The chief called me in for a talk.

The Chief: "This Brother Lucas. You knew him before?"

Me: "We went to high school together."

Chief: "Personal friend?"

Me: "More like an acquaintance."

He stared out the window, not sure how to get into this.

I decided to help him. "Sir, I guess it looks funny, my telling him where to look."

He grunted. I went on.

"Like maybe, if I knew so much, maybe I put it there?"

He grunted again. His grunts were very expressive.

I said, "Here's what I did. I put myself in the mind of the thief. I know the chapel will be searched by experts. So where can I hide it? I think of Poe's "The Purloined Letter.""

"Who? What?"

"In Poe's story the thief hid the letter by leaving it in plain sight – with junk, in the waste basket. It was beautiful. The Paris detectives tore the room apart, and never found it."

"Are you telling me the cup was in plain sight? No, don't answer that. I don't want to know." He sighed and shook his head. "Schultz has called for an Internal Affairs review. No way to sidestep it. Anything you want to tell me before the hearing?"

"Just that you have nothing to worry about. I look forward to the hearing, sir."

He grunted. "Hope Brooks agrees with you."

He referred to Inspector Ira Brooks, Chief of Internal Affairs. Brooks was perfect for the job. He had an almost demonic faculty of getting into the head of the alleged miscreant. He was hated, he was feared. Before coming to Fort West he had been a justice of the peace, working a speed trap on Highway 80 in cooperation with the local sheriff. Before that he had been with the M.P.s serving the Judge Advocate General. And before that he had been a guard in the dynamo room at Huntsville Penitentiary. He did not consider himself a sadist, nor indeed, that he fit any of the names he was called behind his back, names that made him smile. He was just doing his job.

To him being an inspector in Internal Affairs was a calling, like being a minister, or maybe a doctor, or lawyer. It wasn't for everyone. No room for sentiment. Not for the weak-hearted, the compassionate, the lily-livered. He had wept twice in his professional career. The first time, tears of mixed rage and frustration, when he had been listening to his radio, alone in his room, when it was announced that the legislature in Austin had abolished the death penalty. The second time, tears of joy, when the Texas Supreme Court declared the abolition unconstitutional.

His first wife had left him for the operator of a chili parlor; his second had simply left him . . . for no reason that he could discern. Very puzzling.

He conducted his hearings in accord with his view of the law: the accused is guilty until proven innocent. It made for brevity.

Schultz and Ebbitts walked in together. I followed. Schultz turned around and smiled at me. He seemed almost happy. "Boy," he whispered, "you are in deep shit."

"This hearing is held," intoned Inspector Brooks, "pursuant to the provisions of City Ordinance 651-a, of 1927, as revised.

"Present are myself, Ira Brooks, Inspector Internal Affairs; John Stahl, Chief of Police; Walter Goodall, Chief of Detectives; Joseph Barnes, Clerk, Detective Bureau; and Detectives Irwin Schultz and Benjamin Ebbitts. The hearing is held for the purpose of determining whether formal charges shall be brought against Mr. Barnes." He nodded to the lady stenographer, who was taking it all down. (Gregg shorthand, I noted. And she was good.) "Notary, will you please swear in Mr. Barnes."

She did. I took the witness chair.

"Mr. Barnes," he said, "you accompanied Detectives Schultz and Ebbitts in investigating a burglary complaint called in by St. Joseph's Sanctuary, on Camp Bowie?"

"Yes sir."

"According to the complaint, a valuable cup had been stolen?"

"Yes sir."

"The three of you searched the premises but didn't find the cup?"

"Yes sir."

"You found no fingerprints?"

"That's correct."

"Detectives Schultz and Ebbitts returned to work, you stayed behind and conferred with a Mr. Luke Gruen, a lay brother of St. Joseph's?"

"Yes sir."

"An acquaintance?"

"Yes sir."

"What did you talk about?"

"He thought the cup might still be in the chapel. He suggested we take another look. So we did."

"But you didn't find it."

"No sir."

"Then, yesterday afternoon you called him back, and you got Detective Schultz on the extension, and you asked Mr. Gruen certain questions. And then, lo and behold, Mr. Gruen went straight to the cup. Right?"

"Essentially, yes sir."

"It has been suggested, Mr. Barnes, that you knew where it was all along."

"Then you were grossly misinformed. Sir."

"But you admit you knew where it was?"

"Yesterday, before I came to work, I had a hunch where it was. But until Brother Lucas actually found it, I couldn't be sure."

"It has been suggested that you worked in concert with one Hans Ziegler, the janitor."

"No sir. I don't know Mr. Ziegler. I've never met him."

"Really? We'll leave that for the moment. Let's go back to your conversation with Mr. Gruen, yesterday afternoon. You recall that?"

"Yes sir."

"So does Detective Schultz. You deliberately wanted him to be a witness, right?"

"Yes sir."

"Well, he was. And he took notes."

"Yes sir. That's fine."

"You said to Mr. Gruen, 'Go back to the screen porch. Look on the bench. There's a glass container there. See if it's graduated in cc's.' You said that to him?"

"Yes sir."

"But he didn't go right away, did he? Instead he replied, 'John Twenty-one, Five.' And you responded, 'Twenty-one, Six.' Right?"

"Yes sir."

"All of which was code to camouflage your deep involvement in the crime?"

"No sir. My only involvement was in finding the Cup."

"But you were both certainly talking in code?"

"No sir. Brother Lucas was citing from the Gospel of St. John: 'We have fished all night, and caught nothing,' meaning that the back porch had already been searched several times without result. And my reply, John Twenty-one, Six, 'Cast your net on the right side of the boat, and you will find some fish,' meant, look once more, and you'll find it, the Cup, that is."

The Inspector paused and thought about that. I could see that biblical quotations troubled him. They seemed out of place in a felony hearing, but he wasn't about to order the word of God stricken from the record. He had been doing so well, and now his face seemed to suggest that he might be losing control.

I thought perhaps I could help him get back on track. "You see, sir, it was just a question of finding the last piece of the puzzle – a good-sized container measuring cc's – cubic centimeters."

They all looked at each other. And I looked at them. I could see I wasn't helping.

Inspector Brooks was trying to think of what to say next, when my boss beat him to it. "I gather this Mr. Gruen actually did go to the porch?"

"Yes sir. And he found a graduated cylinder on the bench, and reported back, and that's when I knew where the cup was."

"Where?" demanded Brooks.

"There was a bucket of cleaning fluid sitting on the bench. The cup was in the bucket."

Schultz broke in. "Now that's most interesting. There was nothing there when I looked." His voice was hard, grim. He stared at me. His eyes spoke volumes. Gotcha.

"It was there," I said. "You just couldn't see it. It was invisible."

Chief Goodall said grimly, "You'd better explain that."

"Yes sir. Ziegler, the janitor, had been working with a bucket of cleaning solution. I had noted containers of carbon tetrachloride and benzene under his work bench. He had evidently made up a mix of the two. A useless expense, actually. But when Brother Lucas found that the pitcher was measured in cc's, it all came together."

"*What* came together?" demanded Brooks.

"Where the Cup was. The graduated container was essential for hiding the Cup. You see, if carbon tet and benzene are mixed in a volume ratio of exactly fifty one to forty nine, the refractive index of the resulting liquid is 1.47, which is the same as that of borosilicate glass. A cup of such glass sitting in that liquid would be invisible."

They all thought about that.

Chief Goodall caught it first. "The cc graduate was the tip-off? The measurements had to be exact, to the cc?"

"Yes sir."

"Damn clever."

Did he mean me or the party who had put the Cup in the bucket? I didn't say anything.

Brooks looked at his notes. "Not so fast. You told Mr. Luke to wrap a wet handkerchief around his face and empty the bucket in the back yard, carefully, and close to the ground. Right?"

"Yes sir."

"Why all the care?"

"Vapors of both solvents are toxic. And he needed a soft surface to empty the vessel so the Cup wouldn't break when it fell out."

"You should have explained this . . . to somebody . . . " Brooks sounded plaintive. "Still a problem here. Dereliction of duty."

Schultz seemed to take heart.

"Sir," I said softly. "Perhaps you're right. On the other hand, I was thinking of the Department. If I might explain . . ."

"Yeah?" The inspector was skeptical but uneasy.

I said, "Suppose we rush out and arrest somebody. The janitor, maybe. It would be all over the paper. With pictures – and the janitor holding up the Cup, and smiling. He would claim he had been cleaning it – left it in to soak, something like that. We look stupid."

"With budget hearings coming up," murmured Chief Stahl. "Hm. Good point. Let it lie."

"Still . . . " demurred Brooks.

"No, wrap it up, Ira. Luke Fifteen, Twenty-four."

Inspector Brooks gave a puzzled nod to the stenographer, who closed her pad. She would probably look it up later.

Chief Stahl saved her the trouble. " 'That which was lost, is found. Let us celebrate.' The parable of the Prodigal. I think we can all get back to work."

I had been lucky. As in most bureaucratic organizations, where human passions sizzle and nerves are laid bare, the line in the Fort West Police Department between a hero and a bum can be thin.

And any celebration was a bit early. As soon as I got out of there, I made a date to return to St. Joseph's. Prior Paul and I needed to talk.

Father Paul

Luke limped in with me into the darkened office of the prior, Father Paul, introduced me, hesitated a moment, then bowed and left.

The old man studied me from across his desk. "Joseph. Yes. Well-named. A special welcome to our Sanctuary, Joseph." His voice was thin, quavering. Even in the few months since Cybele's death his deterioration was apparent. His eyesight seemed worse, his larynx was behaving erratically, and arthritis in his knees and ankles now confined him to a wheelchair.

"The name is pure coincidence, Father."

"Doubtless." He worked at clearing his throat. It took a long time. "You found the Cup, and we thank you. And now you come in your official capacity." It was both a statement and a question.

"Father Paul, do you want to call your attorney?" I realized that I had adopted the dry monotone of a policeman about to make an arrest.

That amused him. He chuckled. "So you think you know everything?"

"Enough. Was Luke involved?"

"No, just I, and Hans, the janitor. Luke knew nothing about it."

"It was dirty pool to involve Ziegler."

"Yes, you're right. But at the time it seemed to be the only way. Are you going to turn me in?"

"No. It's my sworn duty to arrest you. But I can't. My . . . wife . . . attended school here. You spoke at her funeral. In the Cup Chapel."

"I know. Cybele Wilson." He exhaled slowly.

"Why did you do it?" I asked.

He sighed. "Money, my son. What else? Back taxes had accumulated to over thirty thousand dollars. The scholarship fund was exhausted. We would have had to sell nearly all the land. The Cup Chapel would have been converted into an office building. The kids would have to be placed in other schools or . . . God knows what."

"You could have sold the Cup."

"You know better than that."

"Yeah. But why steal the Cup and then have Luke tell me I knew where it was? That doesn't make sense."

"It looks strange, agreed. Yet it does make sense. Take it step by step. Did you know she had insurance?"

"No."

"She had a sizable policy with Aetna, with the Sanctuary as beneficiary."

"So?"

"There was a delay in payment. A question of whether she had concealed a pre-existing condition, her kidney cancer, you know. They finally decided in our favor. Quite unexpected." From an envelope on his desk he took a check and pushed it over to me. "It came in the mail that same morning, just hours after I reported the theft. I had to . . . correct . . . the situation."

I read it and passed it back. It was for thirty thousand dollars. "Quite a coincidence."

"I agree."

"So you blundered. Your theft was highly premature. So why didn't you just call the Department and say it was all a mistake, that you had merely misplaced the Cup?"

"I almost did. But then I thought, we will look very stupid. And by the time I figured out how to handle the problem, you and the detectives were on your way out here. No, the Cup had to be found right away, but by very scientific police techniques. And by you."

"Why *me?* And what made you so sure I'd find it by scientific police techniques?'"

"I thought it likely *she* would help you."

I stared at him, took a deep breath. I needed time to figure this out. "She was in school here several years. Did you know her well?"

"As well as an old man could know a child. She was special. She was in my science class. I once taught here, you know. We talked a lot."

"You taught chemistry?"

"Yes." He smiled at me. It was a profound, knowing smile, bountiful, yet veneered with a mystic sadness. That smile was speaking to me, but I couldn't quite figure out what it was telling me. Or maybe I didn't want to know.

I shrugged.

He said, "You don't believe in miracles?"

"No. Do you?"

"I have never doubted."

I laughed wryly. "Maybe you're right. She was indeed determined to keep you out of jail."

"Ah. Do you realize the implications of what you just said? In your own mind, you believe she foresaw that you would come here to accuse me.'"

"That doesn't necessarily follow, not at all." But I thought, she certainly did simultaneously save the Sanctuary and this old rascal. How do I explain that?

Father Paul was watching me, and he was greatly amused. I concluded righteously, "In any case it was mean of you to involve Ziegler."

He shook his head. "No, he was never in real trouble. If your Detective Schultz had found the cup, Hansi was to say that he had been cleaning it, and had simply forgotten about it. Actually, we thought there was no chance of that. And we were right. But you, with Cybele's assistance, were sure to find it. Would you care to explain how you worked it out? It shouldn't matter now."

He was right, but I wasn't going to tell him about Cybele and *The Invisible Man* and the back row on the Palace balcony. So I gave him pretty much the same story I had given at the Internal Affairs hearing.

He took it all in. "Very clever."

"Now," I said, "do you want the rest? What I *didn't* tell them?"

He cocked his head suspiciously at me. "Well, why not."

"I didn't tell them it was a fake, that it was a plain Pyrex cup, that borosilicate glass had been around for only a few decades."

I let him chew on that for a few minutes. "And yet," he said, "it produces miracles."

"You say."

"*They* say. You've seen the crutches. Joseph, there's something you have to understand about relics. The *relic* doesn't do the work; it could care less. It's the faith of the worshiper that opens the door to that other world. The relic is – shall we say – just a reference point. Like a surveyor's stake – a place to start. But you wouldn't understand. You have no faith."

"My daddy used to tell me, faith is believing in things that ain't so."

He laughed. "Well, maybe you don't need any, with Cybele as your guardian angel."

"No, that's crazy. I'm an agnostic, Father. I loved her dearly, but I doubt the existence of angels, guardian or otherwise."

"Yes, I see. An agnostic . . . science versus the whole program . . . God . . . Jesus . . . angels . . . miracles . . . the supernatural . . . heaven . . . hell. You neither believe nor disbelieve. The cautious middle road."

I raised my eyebrows. "So?"

We were silent while he took a deep breath. He said, "May I tell you a fable?"

"Sure."

"A great explorer lifted his eyes and scanned the horizon, far and wide, in all directions, looking for the North Pole. But he never found it, because he was standing on it."

That didn't make any sense. I got him back on the subject. "Was there ever a *real* cup?"

"Oh, of course there was. In fact, it was in existence until fairly recently. I saw it in 1915. You want the history?"

"Brother Lucas mentioned some things. He got the history as far as the Middle Ages."

"Let's back up a little. After our St. Joseph died and was buried in Glastonbury, in 72 A.D., the cup was moved at least twice, once to an isolated Benedictine monastery near Canterbury, founded by St. Augustine in 597, later to the Canterbury cathedral. Christianity was spreading rapidly in Britain, but might well have been wiped out by invading Danes and Saxons but for Alfred. He saved the Cup, and turned it over to the Order of St. Joseph. A special branch of the Order was created during the English civil wars for the specific purpose of guarding the Cup, and we, the Keepers of the Cup, brought it safely through Cromwell's desecrations, and it was not again in danger until the Great War."

"What did it *really* look like?"

"Oh, actually rather a simple affair. A glass pot, about the size of our present Pyrex, and decorated with flower petals. It had been blown in a mold. The technique was just coming into fashion in Jesus's day. Glassmaking was a flourishing industry in Jerusalem at the time. But you're right about Pyrex. They couldn't have made it. No borax in the area. What did it look like? It's fairly accurately represented in a relief plaque on the tomb of Archbishop Theodore, sixth century, in Ravenna. Almost, but not quite. And there's that oddity about the blood." He held up a thin forefinger.

"Oh?"

"There's a tradition . . . I'm sure you've heard it . . . during the Crucifixion, Joseph . . . or someone . . . held the Cup under the Cross, and caught drops of blood. That's why Galahad, Percival, and other observers thought the Cup had a crimson cast. Be that as it may, it is known that infrared radiation from a nearby human being will or at least did in other days – induce a certain luminosity in the Cup. This luminosity apparently increased over the years with the number of persons, and toward the end, the impact was apparently sufficient to injure sinful eyes. For this and other reasons the Brothers kept it shut away in a box."

How much of this was true, I wondered. "So what finally happened to it – to the real Cup?"

"Lost at sea. Damn shame. Ironic, really. 1915. The German zeppelins were bombing London, our original home. The Brothers of St. Joseph were frightened. We packed it up and put it on the *Manchester,* a fast liner bound for New York. It was torpedoed. I thought we were going to die . . ."

"So you opened the box. You looked at the Grail."

"Actually, the box was broken open in the explosion, and yes, I did see the Cup. And just before the Atlantic Ocean crashed down over me there was a blinding light. I lost it. But I saw it, Joseph, the real thing. It lies now over a thousand miles east of New York, and several miles down, in what some call the Mid-Atlantic Ridge. Act of God, right? We were picked up almost immediately. But I had seen it. After that it was just a question of . . . shall we say . . . replacing it."

Somehow, I did believe him. But Act of God? Not that part.

He continued. "Seeing the true Grail does strange things to the mind. It closes some eyes, opens others. Some of us are given the gift of prophecy, and the gift of continuing contact with certain of our loved ones." He paused here for a moment, and he smiled that strange Mona Lisa smile. "The Cup sat on her coffin, Joseph. The Cup – and Cybele – will bring you a miracle. Yes, a miracle."

"Hmpf."

He ignored me. "As you know, Joseph, we here are neither Catholic nor Protestant, nor anything in between. Great distances separate us from other religions. Our miracles are unique, peculiar to our order. Certain beliefs of the very early Christian heretics – the Gnostics and Manichaeans – find shelter with us. Buddhism and Hinduism are part of our heritage, and indeed, long before that, certain aspects of Egyptian religion. I refer particularly to metempsychosis – or, in the common tongue, reincarnation. You are smiling?"

I straightened my face and made a sincere effort to rejoin the conversation in a knowledgeable fashion. "Father, I have to agree, the concept of reincarnation has been around for a long time. The German literati – Goethe, Lessing – took it seriously. During the Renaissance, Giordano Bruno held firmly to the idea, and so the Inquisition burnt him at the stake."

"An early martyr," murmured Father Paul.

I said, "The trouble with the whole idea is, there's no real proof."

He met that with a thin cackle. "Quite right. And with good reason."

"Which is?"

"When it happens, those involved . . . *know.* And that's quite sufficient. In fact, they are *forewarned.*"

This was becoming really insane. And I had stepped right into it. "Forewarned? How?"

"The little winged creatures, Joseph. *You* know."

"The . . . ?" I sat up straight.

"Butterflies . . . Think *symbols,* Joseph. Throughout Europe, for millennia the soul was symbolized by the butterfly. In Attic Greek, *psyche* means soul and/or butterfly."

"Moths?" I muttered. "Same thing?"

"Ah, I see. A flight of moths, and Cybele? Yes, it was, and it will be. It will be. Sad, sad, but glorious, my son. Marvelous." He was watching me intently with that queer half-smile. "When the child comes, think of these moments."

What is he trying to tell me? I thought. To him, in some strange (symbolic – ?) way it makes sense. But to nobody else. That's the trouble with mystics: they just can't communicate in a normal way with normal people. Far be it from me to remind him that as yet I had no child. And in fact that I wasn't even married.

He said, "And now a final matter." I watched him fumble at something on his lapel. He was unfastening some sort of ornamental pin. He finally got it loose and pushed it over to me. "Pick it up."

I did. It appeared to be a simple metal leaf, maybe bronze, maybe gold.

"It's a leaf from St. Joseph's Crown of Thorns cutting, at Glastonbury. Bronzed, then gold-plated."

I covered a yawn. "Interesting." I pushed it back.

"It is her wish that you take it."

Is? I thought. "No." He was making that up.

"It's not for you. It's for your wife. It may help her when her time comes."

He was talking crazy again. I had to get out of there. I picked up the pin. I got half way out of the chair, then sat back down. "One last question?"

He gave me a quirky grin. "Like, are Brother Lucas's stigmata genuine? Laid on him by supernatural forces – which you don't believe in?"

He was perceptive, I'll give him that. "Well?"

He sighed. "Good question, Joseph. We're not sure . . . His case is being studied by the High Councilors. No answer yet, maybe never. There may be a mental autocomponent."

"In other words, he wants it so bad, he consciously or unconsciously makes his body erupt?"

"Perhaps. Or even simpler, it may be merely the consequence of refusing treatment for his old phosphorus lesions."

"On his *back?*"

"Self-flagellation, perhaps?"

Again that casual, enigmatic shrug. "Statistics are against him. You are perhaps aware that cases of the complete seven stigmata are extremely rare. Only three or four cases known. Most had only two or three, some only one – the crown or the wound in the side." He paused, smiled faintly. "Supernatural? Time may provide an answer."

"How's that?"

"He may be involved in bringing forth a miracle."

That did it. I said goodbye and left. We parted friends, I think. Sort of.

A puzzle: if that *ersatz* Cup was so powerful, why hadn't it cured Father Paul's eyes, or at least his arthritis? Hah?

The aftermath. You can't keep this sort of thing secret. The Cup had been lost, Brother Lucas (according to the accepted version) had found it, and some people considered *that* a Miracle. And so they came to St. Joseph's: the religious, the skeptical, the curious. Some days the traffic was so bad they had to close off the Chapel. Then the visitors left things at the gatehouse: money, potatoes, Bibles, money . . . It piled up. They trampled the yards. They carried away bits of turf, especially from behind the chapel where Brother Lucas had poured out the solvent mix.

The Head Abbot came down from New York and held torchlight baptismal ceremonies on the banks of the Trinity River. He put up a sign, "Fishers of Men," and was nearly arrested by the Tarrant County sheriff for fishing without a license.

Reporters and photographers drove out from the *Star-Telegram* and the *Press,* and in fact, from all over.

Chief Stahl tried to figure some way to get into the act, but he was never able to get a handle on the religious overtones, and when his campaign manager pointed out that both Catholics and Protestants (combined voter registrations, 38,436) hated and feared the adherents of St. Joseph's (voter registrations, 57) he decided anonymity was the better part of valor.

Sandt and Haber

The dust had barely settled on the Cup Caper when I got a strange call from Diana Mulligan. "Sandt's dying," she explained matter-of-factly. "Doc gives him a day, no more. He's out of his head, keeps calling for a chemist named Fritz. He wants to confess. Something terrible he did years ago."

"He wants a minister? A priest?"

"No. It has to be somebody named Fritz. But maybe you can fill in? You went to seminary?"

"Yeah – but a chemist named Fritz?"

"He just lies there muttering. Something about a cable. 'Warn them,' he says. 'Still time.' He's crazy, Joe. Can you help?"

I thought, how do I get involved in these things? "Okay, Di. Do this. Call Brother Lucas, at St. Joseph's. Tell him Bernard Sandt, Cybele's father, is dying and wants a last communion. Tell him to come to your place, to the Big House, and to bring the Cup. He'll know what I'm talking about. I'm on the way."

I considered the calendar. September 20. I seemed to recall something Di had told me earlier. Every year on September 20 the old man had a fit of depression so severe that he took to his bed. Did it have something to do with the fall equinox? Nobody knew. He refused to talk about it. Whatever it was, it was tied in somehow to chemistry and chemists. He hated chemists. That's why Di never told him about Cybele, until the end. In years past he'd stay sick a day or two and then he'd get up. Apparently this time he wasn't going to get up.

One of the girls met me at the door and took me upstairs to Di's room. I was immediately uneasy. Cybele had died here. Is this where you come to die?

The shades were drawn. It was murky inside, with a ten-watt table lamp on the dresser barely illuminating a scattered collection of bottles and pill boxes.

He lay in Cybele's death bed.

I took a deep breath.

Di whispered, "I told him Fritz was coming. You are Fritz."

"Fritz *who?*" I whispered back.

Sandt called out in a weak gurgle. "Haber? That you, you son of a bitch?"

Then I had it. Fritz Haber. The great chemical genius whose nitrogen fixation process at Oppau had kept Germany in the War and had subsequently put Sandt's Chile nitrate business on the skids. I had read up on the Haber process during my nitrogen fixation project with Cybele at JimBowie High. The Nazi purges had driven the famous Nobelist from Germany, and he had recently died in Switzerland.

I walked over to the bed. And now a weird thing happened. I said with high Teutonic dignity, *"Ich heisse Herr Doktor Fritz Haber. Was wünschen Sie?"* I'm Dr. Fritz Haber. What do you want?

I knew a few German words, but nothing like this. Even my accent sounded authentic. Strange things were going on in my brain. I knew how the disciples felt, at the Pentecost, speaking in tongues. I noted a sudden floral odor, growing stronger. Bluebonnets, of course.

"Speak English, dammit!" gasped the prone man.

"Natürlich, mein Herr."

"Okay. Now listen. I'm dying. Not much time . . ."

"Ach, dass tut mir leid . . ."

"Shut up and listen. I want you to read something. I have written it all out." He dug under the sheets and pulled out a sheaf of papers. "Read it. Out loud."

I looked over at Di. She shrugged, indicating it was a complete mystery to her, too. I took the papers from Sandt's agitated fingers, bent closer to the table lamp, cleared my throat, and began. The beginning was apparently actually in the middle, but no matter. After a while it began to make sense.

" 'After the war the Germans didn't turn off the prilling towers, where sprays of liquid ammonium nitrate droplets fell through hot air and dried into little seed-size prills. The nitrate just kept piling up. By 1919 the pile had become just one enormous monolithic block of nitrate, big as a city block, four stories high. When the peacetime fertilizer market reopened, they tried to haul it away in trucks and railroad cars, but they found that the prills had fused together. To break it up into manageable hunks, they used light explosives. They were very careful about this, and they knew the risk, and they calculated exactly what the charge should be without blowing the whole pile. For over two years everything worked nicely. And they brought our Chile nitrate consortium to the edge of bankruptcy, because the synthetic nitrate was a lot cheaper. The British controlled the Chile consortium. Our Action Committee met in London in 1920. We voted. Conning, the chairman, had lost a son at Ypres, 1915, when the Germans turned three thousand cylinders of chlorine loose into the British trenches. Chlorine was Fritz Haber's fancy idea, you know. A hell of a way to die, really. And here's Haber again, with his synthetic nitrate, destroying Conning the father. We voted. I voted no, but they had the votes. The plan was quite simple. The British agent would substitute TNT for the little gunpowder shots they were using to break up the solid nitrate. Same size, same label, same electrical attachments. It worked. The death toll was in the hundreds. The blast shook towns five hundred kilometers away. The Germans never knew what had gone wrong.

" 'So the consortium had their monopoly once more. But it didn't last. Haber rebuilt the plant, and in five years they had driven Chilean caliche off the market. I didn't care anymore, because I had sold out. No more foreign stuff. I put it all in U.S. stocks.

" 'Did *I* cause the big blast? No. So why do I feel guilty? Because I could have stopped it. A short cablegram. I once wrote it out. But I didn't send it. I did nothing. All those lost souls. Men, women, children. They will be waiting for me, out there. What shall I tell them?' "

I finished. I refolded the papers and handed them back to Sandt.

He looked up at me with bright burning eyes. Some words floated out in a harsh whisper. "Well, Fritz. There it is. And I'm sorry." His face twisted in pained remembrance.

I knew we could not let him die this way, destroyed by guilt for something he didn't do. We owed it to Di, if not to him. We would let him die in peace and dignity. We.

There was a noise behind me, and whispers. Brother Lucas had arrived. It was time to start. I turned back to Sandt. *"Ach, mein lieber Herr Sandt, was Sie sagt, dass ist unmöglich,* ganz *unmöglich."* (I knew Di was looking at me in the semidark, bewildered.)

"Impossible? What do you mean, impossible? Speak English!"

"Ja natürlich, auf Englisch. Impossible because it *explodiert* – exploded – the day before. *Ein grosses Gewitter* – thunderstorm. *Blitz* – lightning – struck. *Ein Schall, ungeheumer gross!"*

"Lightning? Lightning blew the pile? You're lying!"

"Nein, mein Freund! Hier!" I looked hurriedly around the room. Ah – there in the chair.

I showed him the front page of the *Star-Telegram.* "It was in the paper – *Berliner Zeitung. Hier. Lesen, ihr selbst.* Read it yourself."

"I can't read German."

"So. Ich lese. I shall read. How you say, okay?" I brought the front page up to my nose. "At 7:30 a.m. on September 19, 1921, lightning from a severe thunderstorm struck the great block of ammonium nitrate stored at Oppau. The resulting explosion killed five hundred and wounded fifteen hundred men, women, and children. Nearby villages –"

He held up a withered hand. "Enough."

I stopped. Di and Brother Lucas were staring at me.

Then we all looked back at the dying man. Sandt was trying to laugh. At least that's what it seemed like to me. It came out as a weird cackle. "Lightning? God did it? I'll be damned! Act of God . . . all this time! Son of a bitch!"

I joined in. "*So. Der lieber Gott hat gesprochen.* God Himself has spoken. *Sie sind ein gutes Mann, Herr Sandt, ein treues Ritter,* a true knight. *Ruhe, Freund.* Rest."

He lay there in silence for several minutes, just breathing hard. Then he whispered: "Fritz, do you think *she* forgives me?"

I looked at Di. We both knew what he was trying to say. "Cybele. *Ja. Cybele ihnen vergibt.* She forgives you."

"Good. I will go now."

"*Warte, bitte.* Wait a bit. The minister has come. He will give you communion." And then, I thought, you can die.

"Well —"

I nodded to Luke. He and Di had been busy at the dresser. He limped forward now, carrying the Cup, about a third full of Di's best Italian red wine. It glittered. I put my arm under Sandt's back and lifted him up. The Cup shone with a strange crimson radiance.

Brother Lucas said, "No bread. He cannot chew. The wine only. And just a wetting of the lips." His voice changed, went into a lower register, almost a monotone. "And Jesus took a cup, and when he had given thanks he said, 'Drink of it, for this is my blood of the covenant, which is poured out for many for the forgiveness of sins.' "

A strange illusion now. The only light in the room was the red radiance from the Cup. The dying man had swallowed nothing. The wine had barely touched his lips. There was a vague trickle on his scrubby unshaven chin. But the wine was gone. All of it. Luke looked at me. I looked at him. Were we amazed? No, not really. He shrugged.

And so, like daughter, like father, he died in my arms. I let him gently back onto the pillow. Di came over and closed his eyes. Hers stayed dry.

The Cup-light dimmed and died. The room was semi-dark again.

Di switched on the ceiling bulb. She was squinting and frowning at me. She said quietly, "I didn't know you spoke German."

"I don't."

"She was here?"

"Yes."

She sighed. "She was his daughter. He never acknowledged her. The only thing I held against him."

"They'll straighten it out now." I walked toward the door. "Luke and I are going down now. We'll send the girls up."

"Tell them to wait a little. Give me an hour."

And that's about it for Bernard Sandt.

Yes, *she* was there. I don't think she would have missed it for anything.

I followed Luke down to the cars. After he had carefully stowed the Cup away in a box on the front seat, I asked him, "Is this what the stigmata is all about? Death?" It was probably the wrong question, but I didn't know the right one.

He stuck his head out the car window and I could see his face in the light of the corner street light. It held a strange smile. "Life," he said. He pushed the starter button.

I spoke over the noise of the motor, "Will I see you again?"

He seemed to think about that a long time before he answered. His face held a faraway look I had never seen before, sort of a glowing sadness. "Yes, one more time. I loved her too, Joe. But she chose you. Goodbye."

He made no sense. "Lukey –"

The car pulled away. Okay, let him take his confounded mysteries with him. I had merely wanted to remind him to change the bandage on his forehead. It was seeping blood.

John Drom

One Friday evening Max Russell, turnkey for the shift, brought two people into the print room.

One was a boy about fifteen, red curly hair atop cherubic face. He was well-known in the Department.

The other was a tall man with deep downcast eyes. I knew him, too. I looked at the arrest ticket. "John Drom." At least he had had the presence of mind not to give his right name.

"Pants down?" I asked Max.

"Yeah, alley next to the Palace. Might as well have been in Washer Brothers' window."

In flagrante delicto. Public nuisance. If held over and tried, ninety days in the County. I grimaced.

Max saw it. "You know him?"

"Yeah." We talked in low voices.

"Shit."

"Yeah." I had to get on with it. I sat at the ancient Underwood and typed in the data on two fingerprint cards. Drom, John. White. 6'. Brown hair, brown eyes. S.C./Vice. And the date. I got up, pushed the cards into the card holders, and spread a little dab of black printer's ink into a thin film over the glass slab. I turned, motioned to him. Very meekly he came over to the print bench.

The boy watched all this in silent amusement.

I hated to touch "Drom." I may have hesitated a fraction of a second before I took his right hand. It was wet with perspiration. I handed him a paper towel. "Dry your fingers. They have to be dry to take the ink."

He dried his hands. I took his hand again. "Relax. Make it limp. Shake it, like this." He did. "No, don't press, don't try to help me."

He sighed. It was half a sob, and his voice shook. "I don't know what came over me."

I was skeptical. A sex offender generally has a considerable record. But of course maybe there's always that first time. First time caught, anyway. Maybe this was it for him.

And so, one by one, I rolled the ten fingers of Dr. Mord. He said in a low voice, "*Two* sets, Joseph?"

"One for us, one goes to the F.B.I."

"In Washington, D.C.?"

"Yes."

"Oh dear. What happens now?"

Interesting question. Evidently his was indeed his first arrest. If he had been in before, he would know what happens next. "I check your prints against the files. If we don't show any priors, the sergeant probably won't file charges, and you'll be out within the hour."

At which time, I thought, you might well encounter the Friday night choir from the Seminary, coming in as you leave. Is this what I want? Well, yes and no. Yes, for revenge. No, for larger reasons. Revenge because you rejected my sermon and canceled my scholarship and humiliated me. And yet, it was a rejection that led to that wonderful night in Forest Park, and Cybele. You deserve the worst; nevertheless, in balance I owe you.

And then, there was Mother. If he were identified here, the news would get around. The consequences would be far-reaching and ultimately devastating . . . in the Seminary . . . in the Church . . . in Christian homes all over the city. Mother wouldn't be able to handle it. And calling on her vast resources of unique female logic, she would probably even blame *me!*

He looked dubiously at his inked fingertips. "Will it come off?"

"Get a paper towel, there. Pour a little gasoline on it, rub your fingers. It comes off, most of it."

A plan was forming. "Did you leave anything at check-in? Wallet? Watch? Anything that could I.D. you?"

"No – just a couple of bills."

"Nothing you have to go back for?"

"No. Well . . . depending . . . bus fare?"

I fished a bus token from my pocket. He took it and groaned softly. "It's hell, Joseph. To be this way. You can't imagine."

I said nothing. I motioned to the boy. "Hi, Chili, how's business?"

He shrugged. "A bad night."

Evidently Mord hadn't paid him.

I put the boy's ticket aside. We already had his prints, taken when he was in grammar school. His rap sheet had over a hundred entries. "Social Services will want to talk to you in the morning."

"Yeah. Supper?"

"You're just in time. Hamburger." I finished up, Max took them both back to the block. I ducked into the darkroom, washed my hands with antiseptic soap, then checked Mord's prints for priors. Nothing. He was clean. I called the desk sergeant. Mord would be discharged in a few minutes.

And now Max and I had to have a quick discussion. I intercepted him on his way back from the block and we walked along together. "I need a favor." I spoke rapidly. "The tall guy was Dr. Mord, one of the big guns at the Seminary."

He stopped.

I said, "The Seminary choir sings in the lock-up on Friday nights."

"Yeah, I know."

"They'll be coming in through the main entrance." I looked at my watch. "Any minute."

Max rubbed his chin. "I can take him out through the garage. Did he have anything at check-in?"

"No. Skip that."

Max studied me with a curiosity tinged with disbelief. "You actually *like* the old pervert?"

"It's my mother, Max. She has a weak heart. She thinks he's Jesus, Tom Mix, Ronald Colman, Lloyd Douglas, all rolled up into one. This could kill her. Listen!"

The choir was in the building, coming into the main hall behind us, and singing *Amazing Grace,* one of Mord's favorites.

Max hurried off toward the tank, rattling his keys. And just in time, for I was certain that I heard, from the bowels of the cell-block, a baritone in mournful harmony, ". . . a wretch like me . . . !"

I stood there for several minutes, thinking about what I had done, trying to sort things out. What I had done was right. I had no doubts about that. But it wasn't simple Christian charity. No, it was much more complicated.

It had been within my power to destroy him. Instead, I had saved his sorry ass. Why? He was worse than Scather. Her, I had secretly lied to, deceived, and mocked. Why not similar treatment for this perverted wretch?

Why? I think I knew the answer, some of it, anyway. Because he was already well into his own destruction and needed no help from me. Yes, I perceived him as teetering at the edge of a cliff. I did not propose to take the blame for any fatal misstep. He would do it himself, all in good time. Did that make sense? Not completely. But then there was that other reason: Mother.

Oh, the hell with it . . . too deep for me . . . leave him to heaven!

Helen

Several weeks later I encountered Helen Dyess standing on a street corner near SCU. She was waiting for the downtown bus. So was I.

The late morning sun caught her in profile. There was something about her dark eyes, the arrangement of her hair, her relaxed posture, that reminded me of some of Mother's early Riverside photos.

She smiled as I walked over.

"Hello, Joe."

"Hi. Going into town?"

"Yeah. You?"

"Me too. What's your schedule for the afternoon?"

She studied me for a moment. "Some research at the Library. Then home."

"I've got a suggestion. Why don't we have a quick lunch at Carters, then take in the Grace Moore movie at the Worth?"

"Sounds interesting."

"But I couldn't take you home. I have to be at work at three."

"That's okay."

Our first date. Semi-date. There were others, at first intermittent, desultory. Then more frequent, and eventually matters became serious.

Helen wasn't Cybele, but she was special, and she helped fill an aching need. We went steady. Our kisses turned ardent. In the privacy of her darkened porch and parlor she accepted my hands on her breasts, thighs, buttocks. It went no farther, but we began to think of the future. I never mentioned Cybele.

And so it was decided. I would go to Washington, work for the government, send money home to Mother, get my degree in chemistry at George Washington University at night. Helen would follow, and we would be married there. She would work.

It all unfolded pretty much as planned. Plus some unplanned things.

When I left Fort West I had to decide how much of my accumulation of twenty-one years to take with me. The clothes were easy. I didn't have much. I pondered what to do with my/her little skipping rock from the Paleozoic, which I had inherited along with the books. I couldn't see much use in taking it to Washington. But I did anyway.

Books were a problem, especially books I had inherited from Cybele. I couldn't take them with me. I couldn't throw them away. Finally I took them all in to Miss Meigs, still librarian at JimBowie, for which she thanked me graciously. The only book I kept was the little New Testament, which I had taken from Cybele's dying hand.

She had a curious habit of writing notes and sticking them into whatever book was handy. I found this one folded up in Partington's *Elements of Chemistry.*

[Cybele's Note]
June 10, 1925

In the years I boarded at St. Joseph's I had a fairly accurate idea of what my mother did for a living. But it was something I had grown up with, and I didn't think much about it one way or another.

Oh, I knew we were different. I had birthday parties, but they were always held at the Sanctuary. The other girls rarely invited me home to meet their parents. I accepted that. In graduation week I didn't have a date for the prom. That didn't surprise me. I could live with that.

So, on June 1 I graduated from high school. I was first in my class. Father Paul handed me my diploma, clasped my hand, looked me hard in the eyes, and told me we would meet again. I had no idea what he meant.

Mother was there in her shiny new Hudson Super-Six, one of the new closed cars, with genuine glass windows you could roll up and down. The dorms were closed for the summer. She didn't want me to stay with her at the Big House. She had reserved a room for me at the Texas Hotel. The following Saturday I was to go on to Washington, D.C., where I would start summer school in George Washington University.

When we drove up to the hotel, I refused to get out. I told her I was coming home with her, to the house on East Second Street.

There was a bit of a scene. Finally she gave up, and we drove on "home." She made up a bed for me in her upper room. It was hot, but there were fans in both windows, and I didn't mind. I stripped down, got into my pink rayon housecoat, and went down into the parlor. I was talking to the girls and waiting for William to grill me a hamburger when the police came with the paddy wagon. It was an unscheduled raid. Mother was indignant, horrified, vocal. Vice had fouled up the dates. She wasn't supposed to be raided until the following Tuesday. Her protests did no good. (Chief Stahl called the next week with profuse apologies for the mix-up and expressed the hope that she would continue to support his re-election in the u$ual way. And so life went on.)

I spent the night in the city jail with the other girls. A policeman took my fingerprints.

I was out the next morning. This time I went to the hotel. I felt a great emptiness. It's hard to describe. I had no home. No father. No mother. I was a whore's bastard whore. Society had defined me. I was on record in the police files. In fact, the matron had told me kindly but firmly that I'd have to check in once a month at the City-County Hospital for tests. She also gave me some hygiene tips useful to a girl just starting out.

Back at the hotel I studied myself in the dresser mirror. I looked hideous. I worked on my hair a little, but it was no use. I sat on the bed and stared at the door. Mother was supposed to meet me in the lobby as soon as she paid the fines and got the girls back to the House.

I took a last hopeless look at the mirror and walked out the door to the elevator. I looked around for her when I stepped out into the lobby. She wasn't there yet.

I kept on walking.

I walked over to Commerce and got on a Hemphill streetcar headed south. Half an hour later, way out on the South Side, I got off and started walking east.

I had decided to die. I wasn't going to bother anybody. I had my bottle of pills, take one at night, for insomnia. I was simply going to disappear, and if and when they found me, I would be dead.

There is a wild, unsettled area in southeast Fort West. It may have a name, I don't know. The land is dotted with undersized oaks and evergreens. A stream runs through it, one of the several local tributaries to the Trinity. The creek beds are full of ancient shells and ammonites. The underlying rocks hereabouts are mostly Cambrian limestone and weathered shale.

I dearly love this place; I have walked along this stream several times. All this land lay under flowing water as recently as half a million years ago. (A blink of the eye in geologic time.) During that submergence, water carved out cavities in the limestone, some big, some little. Then the land rose again, and what was left has a name: Karst topography. In Kentucky, it gave Mammoth Cave; in New Mexico, Carlsbad Caverns; in Virginia, Luray Caverns.

My little creek didn't border anything so impressive. Still, what it had was adequate. It gave me my very own limestone cave, in the side of a little cliff bordering the creek. The cave mouth was small – you had to enter on your hands and knees. I kept it covered with dead branches to conceal it and to keep out bats and other varmints.

So now I pulled the camouflage away, crawled inside, and waited for my eyes to adjust to the semi-darkness. I looked around. Nothing had changed since my last visit.

My intended burial chamber was roughly cubical, about 8 by 8 by 8 feet. A single stalactite hung from the middle of the ceiling, and it joined solidly with a stalagmite rising from the floor. Water, falling drop by drop, had made this calcium carbonate artifact thousands of years ago.

I sighed, gathered my skirts under me, and sat down with my back to the pillar. I would sit here, and I would die here. I touched the bottle of pills in my skirt pocket, just to make sure it was still there. Not yet, not yet. I felt very sorry for myself. Tears gathered in my eyes. I cried a little. Then I put my head down on my knees, and I guess I dozed off.

I don't know what woke me up. In fact, I'm not sure you could call it being awake.

A figure was standing there, outlined by the light from the cave entrance. I knew right away who it was. Father Paul, from St. Joseph's. When he saw he had my attention, he sat down on the floor in front of me and crossed his legs under his robe, yogi fashion. He did this easily, gracefully. I was surprised, because I knew he had bad arthritis in his knees.

He smiled at me. "You called?"

"Yes, Father. I'm going away. I'm going to die here. I wanted to say goodbye. And can you say goodbye to my mother for me."

"As you wish."

"I don't really want to die, Father, but everything is wrong. Everything hurts."

"How do you plan to do it?

"Sleeping pills. Do you know any reason I shouldn't?"

"Because you're too smart."

"Irrelevant. Nobody loves me."

"Your mother loves you. I love you."

"I'm a woman, Father. I'm seventeen. With all respect, I want a man with hormones to love me. I want a passionate young man to say to me, 'Cybele, I love you, with all my heart, with all my soul and body, forever and ever.' What I want from him, *need* from him . . . I'm afraid to tell you. You would be shocked."

"Nothing shocks me, Cybele."

"All right then. Help me find him. I'm not pretty. My figure is questionable. I'm not glamorous. I need something special. What can you give me?"

"A scent, a special perfume, which only you will have. You can turn it on and off, like a light. You'll know when to use it, and on whom."

"On *him?*"

"On him."

"So where is he?"

"He will come, child. Rachel waited a long time for Jacob."

"I'll be an old woman! I want him *now*. Where is he, Father Paul? Hah! You see? You're just making this up!"

"No. I give you my solemn word. He exists. He's alive. He's younger than you, but when the time comes, that won't matter to either of you. He will give you his complete love – all that he has . . . his body, his mind, his spirit. What will *you* give *him?*"

"Why everything . . . of course . . . all my love, till I die."

"And *after?*"

"And after. But –"

"Go forth. Make your own way. You will find him. And remember, he is also searching for you. And now I must go."

"But Father, where is he?"

"There." And so saying, Father Paul faded away.

My cave entrance darkened. Someone had crawled in. The intruder stood up inside. I could see that he was a boy, maybe ten or twelve. He was apparently waiting to adjust to the darkness. I could see his form, but not his face.

For a moment there was absolute total silence. You could hear the stream gurgling softly, ten yards away.

I started to get to my feet, but at the very first sound my visitor gasped, whirled, and disappeared through the cave-mouth. For a few seconds I heard him splashing upstream, then all sounds ceased.

Well, Father Paul, bless us all. Life had suddenly become interesting again.

The lad had dropped something – an ancient shell. As a souvenir of the occasion I recovered it.

Back to reality. And to poor Mom. Stood up. I wondered if the cops were out looking for me. When I finally got to a phone, she was too relieved to scold me. And actually we did have supper together next day at the T & P Station, and then I boarded the train headed for Washington, D.C.

That scene with Father Paul was all hallucination, of course. Rather like a dream, where the dreamer reconstructs a long involved action sequence from a single sensory event, such as a train whistle, or the tingling of an alarm clock. I must have created the whole fantasy from that boy's ten-second intrusion. We all know that our beloved Prior had strange powers, but hardly that strange, and hardly that powerful.

And that concludes Cybele's note.

I read it a couple of times before I destroyed it.

So – she had deliberately met me in Forest Park that fateful night. As laid out by Father Paul, I was her destined lover. The boy in the cave, full grown and ardent when his time came.

Was this all there was to it? Girl finds boy. Was it as simple as that?

No – there had to be more: something that she knew (or thought she knew) that I did not know. Was I to be just a lover, or was there something more, a thing I – only I – could give her? A vague gift, hovering out of reach, out there in the shadows. Frustrating . . . and just a little frightening. And ironic. Dead, she was telling me more than when she had been alive. But still not everything. She had foreseen her death. What else had she foreseen? What is the rest of the story?

On my last day at the P.D., when I was saying my goodbyes, I looked up at Schultz. He was in the blotter room having coffee and doughnuts at the card table with his partner and a couple of other plainclothes. Somebody – it looked like Lieutenant Parlette – was trying to burn a sugar lump in a saucer, but the lump was not cooperating. I had a sudden inspiration. I was about to make a magnanimous gesture, thereby possibly wreaking utter confusion in the mind of Irwin Schultz. I went over, pulled him out of the group, and asked quietly. "Do you want to know the trick?"

He looked at me suspiciously. I knew he wanted very much to know, but I also knew it would hurt his pride to ask. So I went ahead anyhow. "The match has nothing to do with it. The trick is, you put a bit of cigarette ash on the sugar. Nobody has to know. Then you put the match flame to the border of the ash on the sugar, and the lump will burn."

He just looked at me, grim, hard, still unbelieving. "Ash? Like hell. Don't jive me, Barnes."

"The ash is a pyrogenetic catalyst. Go on, try it. You have everything you need over there." To make it convincing, I began to lie. The temptation was just too great. "This trick would cost you fifty dollars in any magic store, and they'd swear you to secrecy. You'd have to sign a form. They say Houdini discovered it in 1906, and sold it to Blackstone. In Texas only eight people know about it. You'll be the only one in the department."

He was still doubtful. "So why are you telling *me?*" He was thinking, of course, of how he had recently tried to get me fired.

Now was the time to pour on the B.S. If there is a special hell for rampant liars, I am headed there. I responded with quiet authority, "Because it's well-known you are the best and smartest detective in the Bureau, and because I'd be greatly honored if I could leave here thinking you were my friend."

It took him a moment to digest that. He worked on it with face and jaws. Finally it was irresistible. He knew he was the best and smartest, and I think it pained him that not everyone could see it. He nodded in confirmation. His eyes opened wide and he almost grinned. "Well, I'll be damned. Wait here."

He returned to the card table. I saw that he was placing a sugar cube in the saucer. Had he remembered to touch it with ashes? Apparently yes, because he was positioning it carefully. He took a new bill from his wallet. I blinked. It was a ten-dollar bill. Hey, this was serious stuff. Who said anything about a wager? And who's he betting? Oh oh! Lieutenant Parlette sneered, pulled out his gold diamond-encrusted Zippo lighter and calmly laid it on the greenback.

I wanted to sink to the floor. Schultz and Parlette had competed for the lieutenancy, but when the exam had been given, Schultz had been in the hospital with a bullet wound. Postponement denied. Politics, some said. Anyhow, contrary to the Christian commandment, they did not love one another.

The Zippo was Parlette's gesture of combined confidence and contempt. His wife had given it to him at a big party, along with his silver Lieutenant's bars. Schultz had been invited but had not attended.

The problem now was that I had never personally tried the trick. I couldn't be sure it worked. I had merely read about it in one of the books Cybele had left me when she died. Schultz was trusting me, and I was trusting somebody who had written a book. This was a lot of trust. Good thing this was my last day in the P.D.

There was total silence in the room. Sergeant O'Leary was on the phone, talking, I think, to Chief of Police Stahl. We heard him whisper, "Can you hold just a minute, Chief . . . little emergency here." He put his hand over the mouthpiece and turned to watch.

Schultz struck his match. Everybody stood back. I began to perspire. He touched the flame carefully to the little cube of carbohydrate. For a moment, nothing. Then it caught, with a strong blue flame.

Schultz laughed wickedly and picked up the loot. Lieutenant Parlette stared in horror.

The winner sauntered back to me, still chuckling. "You're okay, kid." He flicked the flint on this new lighter, which flamed up nicely. "Y'all come back and see us once in a while."

So I travelled East. To Washington, D.C., The Bureau of Mines, chemistry at George Washington University, and a new world.

The Bureau of Mines

The day I arrived in Washington I checked in at the YMCA, and I stayed there a couple of days while I explored, looked for a place to live, and made ready to report to work.

L'Enfant had laid out the city streets with precision. Everything made sense. I didn't need a map, but of course I got a couple anyhow.

It turned out that there were two Department of the Interior Buildings, one old, one new, a block apart, separated by a reflecting pool bordered by benches and dwarf pink magnolias. Washington is full of pools, fountains, and formal gardens, and the block between those two buildings was one of the prettiest.

The next day was Sunday, and after a light lunch at a nearby White Tower, I walked over to the Interior Reflecting Pool and sat down on the edge of the pool wall and looked across the water.

I noticed then that I had something in my jacket pocket. I pulled it out. It was a shell, in fact my little skipper, Champ. I must have put it in my pocket and then forgot it.

And suddenly I was homesick. It's hard to describe. Not nausea. More like a pain crawling around in my gut, trying to get out.

I tossed the shell in the air, caught it, tossed it again.

The pain ebbed.

Somebody was talking to me. A kid, a boy maybe ten, twelve years old, standing there. I noted then, a few yards behind us, a gray-haired man sitting on a bench and reading a paper. I hadn't noticed him before. Evidently he and the boy had just arrived. He knew we were there, but wasn't really paying much attention.

The boy repeated, "Whatcha got?"

It all came to me in a flash. How to pass a Sunday morning. "You don't recognize it?" I asked incredulously.

"No. What is it?"

I shook my head sadly. "Really surprised they didn't teach you in school. Well, it's the famous San Jacinto skipping stone."

"The *what?*"

(The gray-haired man was watching us curiously over the top of his newspaper. He could hear everything.)

"You'd have to be from Texas to understand."

"I know about Texas. We had Texas in school."

"You did? Well, okay, I guess I can tell you. It goes way back, when Texas was part of Mexico. The Texans got together and held a revolution, and broke away from Mexico. The Mexicans didn't like that at all, so they sent their best general, Mr. Santa Anna, to persuade the Texans to give up on their revolution, and stay in Mexico. With me?"

"Yeah."

"Well, the Texas sent *their* best general, Mr. Sam Houston, to talk to Mr. Santa Anna and persuade *him* to turn around and go back to Mexico City. The two men met on the banks of the San Jacinto River, April 21, 1836, just over a hundred years ago. The San Jacinto is a nice little river a few miles east of where the city of Houston is today."

I gathered momentum. "Well, they had a long discussion. That didn't decide anything. Then they agreed they'd have some sort of contest, winner to take Texas. At first, they were going to play one game of chess, and they actually made up a board using Santa Anna's checkered table cloth. But then they couldn't find any chessmen. And then they talked about drawing high card from a deck of cards, but they couldn't agree on whose deck to use, and there were hints and insinuations of cheating, aces up sleeves, that sort of thing. It got nasty, and they almost came to blows.

"While all this was going on, soldiers on both sides were skipping rocks and shells all over the San Jacinto River, and laughing, and making wagers whose rock would make the most bounces.

"That's it! The two great generals got the same idea at the same time. They would hold a rock-skipping contest. They would call it the Battle of San Jacinto, and the general whose rock bounced the most times over the river would take title to all of Texas.

"So everybody went down to the river bank. Santa Anna picked up several small flat rocks, one after another, handling them, getting the feel, until he found the very one he wanted.

"Then Sam Houston did the same. As you must have guessed by now, this little stone is the very one *he* chose."

The kid said, "Can I touch it?"

"Not yet. Wait till I finish."

"Sure, go on."

"Well, Santa Anna said, 'I go first. And Houston said, 'It's your privilege, since you're a guest on Texas soil.'

"Now the great Mexican general didn't like that, and he sort of glowered, and he may have said something nasty, in Spanish. Then he said, 'Stand back.' And everybody stood back.

"They noted then that he was holding his rock exactly right, between thumb and forefinger . . . like so." (I demonstrated.) "And the Texans realized then that maybe they had walked into a trap. But it was too late.

"Santa Anna wound up, just like Walter Johnson on the mound. He knelt down, to get a narrow angle on the water. He threw. The rock bounced on the water . . . and bounced . . . and bounced . . . until you thought it would never stop. For a total of seven very good bounces. It was clearly a record. There were great gasps on both sides.

"So the happy Mr. Santa Anna faced General Houston (who stood there, trying not to show how worried he was), and he said, 'General Houston, I will spare you the humiliation of throwing your sorry little rock. Now begone! Go back to Tennessee, before I have my soldiers arrest you!'

"But ole Sam just smiled his famous smile. 'Just one little ole cotton-pickin' minute, amigo. It ain't over yet.' And here the Texans turned to their champion in mingled hope and anxiety. Sam Houston laughed out loud. He took two steps to the water's edge, and the rest was a blur. All you could see were splashes across the water."

The kid's eyes were bugging out. "How many?"

"Eight. Maybe nine. There was an argument about the last one. Anyhow, Houston's rock didn't sink at the end. It bounced out on the other side of the river. The Texans recovered it, and for a long time they kept it on display in the capital building in Austin."

"So how come *you* have it?"

"I'll tell you. It's all according to legend. After one hundred years, it has to be returned to water, far away from Texas. Otherwise the state will have one hundred years of bad luck. They gave it to me to bring here. I was about to toss it into the pool when you showed up."

"Oh."

"April 21 is a big holiday in Texas," I said. "It's called Skipping Day. All the schools let out, and the kids hold rock skipping contests."

A pause.

I said, "You ever skip a rock on the water?"

"No. Is it hard?"

"Easy as pie. Here, take it. Hold it . . . like so." I showed him. "All you have to do is spin it and throw it at the same time. Okay?"

"Me?"

"Sure. It's got to go into the water today, one way or the other. Just make sure nobody's on the other side of the pool."

"Nobody's there." He threw. It made eight good bounces, then sank. He danced up and down. "Wow!"

I noted then that the gray-haired man had folded his paper and now stood behind us. He smiled in a way that convinced me he wasn't used to it. "Very educational," he said dryly. "We thank you for the demonstration, but I'm afraid we have to go now. Come along, Billy."

The kid turned to go. "Mister, is *any* of that true?"

I showed I was hurt. "Would a Texan *exaggerate?*"

"You mean, *lie?*"

I didn't reply.

He laughed and ran over to a car that had just then pulled up at curbside, followed by the senior citizen.

I turned back to the pool. The ripples were gone. The surface was mirror-smooth.

I saw then the reflection. A woman standing behind me, and laughing, except there was no sound. My heart began to hammer at my chest walls. It pounded in my ears. My knees turned to jelly. I sort of collapsed. My hands grabbed at the pool wall, and I sat on it, and panted, and stared at her face on the water. Oh, Cybele, Cybele, with bluebonnets!

I knew that if I turned around she'd be gone. So I sat very still, not even blinking. And the memories came flooding back. I held her naked body once more in Forest Park, and in her car, her apartment, her death-bed, many many strange times and places. And I knew it was all wrong, because I was engaged to be married to a very real flesh and blood sweetheart.

Oh Cybele! I *know* we promised to be together forever. I'll never forget that. It was beautiful. But now you're dead. It's over. We must accept it. Life goes on.

Finally, I turned around. Nobody there, of course. Then I looked back at the pool. Gone from there, too.

It was a cool day, but I was perspiring copiously.

I went over to the other side of the pool, rolled up my sleeve, and fished the shell out.

As I walked back to the Y, holding the wet shell in my hand, I was still thinking. I had read Bram Stoker's *Dracula*. I knew vampires didn't reflect in mirrors. But this was just the opposite. Her sainted flesh wasn't there, but her reflection was.

The next Monday morning when I reported to work in the Bureau of Mines in the new Interior building, the personnel lady took me around and introduced me to certain people I'd be working with and/or for, including the head boss, Section Chief Dr. Henry Schaefer.

As we shook hands he spoke first, in his dry embarrassed voice, "Ah, the Texan."

All those lies. But I could tell he wasn't mad at me, just puzzled. (It stayed pretty much that way for the next several years.)

"Yes sir," I said.

He asked the personnel lady, "Where are we assigning Mr. Barnes?"

"To the clerical pool, for the time being."

"Perhaps we should skip that. Mr. Barnes has certain talents."

"Oh?" she said. (I was puzzled, too.)

"Let's try Mr. Barnes with MAW."

"Oh?" She was really puzzled, now. Me too.

"MAW, '*Minerals Around the World,*' Mr. Barnes. Our little monthly magazine. Rather stodgy at present. Could use some new blood . . . factual, but with a *human* . . . touch. Eh?"

Yep. Dr. Henry Schaefer . . . the gray-haired man on the bench. Actually rather famous in his field. He had come to work that Sunday morning, and had brought his grandson. Afterwards, they had waited at the pool for grandma to pick them up.

I could understand how he hadn't known what to do with the kid. He worked seven days a week for the government, and it had bent him and blanched his face and hair. I had an idea how bored the kid had been. The boy's father was in the Navy, and out of the picture.

Dr. Schaefer had a beautiful face, the kind you could put on a Boy Scout calendar. He belonged to another century, when it was still okay to have ideals and believe in a lot of neat stuff, like the Ten Commandments, the American system (whatever *that* was), the Methodist Church, and the Republican party. He had survived the Great War and roller coaster rides with in-and-out political parties (presently Rooseveltian, but he was biding his time). He was sufficiently important to be able (due proceedings had) to fire some sixty underlings (including me) – but yet too far below the frothing hierarchal surface to be fired himself, so long as he stayed out of the papers. Sort of like a squid, living quietly on the ocean bottom, eating slow-moving life, untroubled by surface storms, but nevertheless watchful for the once-in-a-lifetime predaceous sperm whale.

MAW didn't pay more money, but it had status and it opened doors. It was sort of like getting a promotion my first day at work. Had Cybele engineered this?

Chemistry

So I enrolled in the chemistry program at George Washington University, with all lectures and labs at night. I attended much the same classes that Cybele had attended years before. I worked in the same labs where she had worked, even at the identical benches. Thus:

On that first night I was one of the first into the general chemistry bay. "Take any bench you like," the instructor said. "First come, first served. And here's a sheet which lists the stuff you should find in your cabinet. Check your equipment . . . test tubes, Florence flask, round-bottom flask, tongs, pneumatic trough, Bunsen, and so on."

I looked around. Which bench? They were all identical. Cybele had had a bench in this very bay. It would be an interesting coincidence if I picked hers. One out of thirty. I walked through the rows, slowly at first, then with growing certainty. Second row, in the middle. I stopped and opened the cabinet. A faint floral odor floated up and caressed my face. My heart quit briefly. I plopped my lab manual down on the bench and leaned over and steadied myself on the hard black surface.

I got myself under fair control and began checking my apparatus list. Everything was there. Time to get to work. The rest was routine. First, shed my jacket. We did this by hanging our jackets on a hook out in the hall, running a chain through a sleeve, then locking the chain back on itself with a combination lock, which would later be placed on our lab cabinet when we closed up for the night.

Later that night, after lab, as I walked the two blocks back to my room, I thought about the "coincidence." Had she known ten years ago that I would select that particular bench? Or had she *guided* me to it tonight? Or both? Or was it simple impossible coincidence? No. Her scent was fresh. Tonight, at 7 p.m., she had been there.

As the years passed I found her bench cabinets in the labs four times in a row. Each of the four bays had thirty lab benches. Each bench had its own sink and faucet, plus drawer and cabinet. At the possessor's pleasure, a shelf could be fastened inside. And like schoolboys carving initials on desks, initials could be cut into the shelves, or in the case of girls, burned in with the tip of a fingernail file heated red hot in a Meker burner. After that first incident in general chem I found "CW" on shelves in organic, in qual, in quant, in phys, in advanced inorg, in advanced org. "CW" always. I didn't even have to search for her benches. With each new semester I walked right up, opened the cabinet door, and there it was, every time.

Whenever I took her bench I sniffed for the scent of bluebonnets. Oh, other smells were there; too: reagents, solvents, oxidants, the works. No doubt about that. And the algebraic sum of the odors was different, lab by lab. I could close my eyes in any lab and know exactly where I was. But her tell-tale perfume floated above it all. She was there.

Calculate the probability/improbability of walking right up to each of the four. Each lab bay had thirty benches. Four labs. $30^4 = 810,000$ chances to guess wrong.

In a casual way I eventually became acquainted with various of my lab neighbors. Most of them (like me) worked for the government in some capacity. Most were in my age group They were earnest, determined, serious. This was our chance to get a science degree in a first-class university, and they – and I – had seized upon it.

A few had outside financial support – perhaps affluent parents or a scholarship – and some of these had night labs.

"Kash" was one of these. "Kash" only approximated his actual name. His surname as entered on the rolls was unpronounceable. His first name was even worse. But he responded well to "Kash." According to rumor he was subsidized by the Czechoslovakian embassy, where his father was supposed to be a high functionary, and on graduation it was assumed that the son would join the embassy as science attache.

We loved Kash – for semi-sadistic reasons. He was so clumsy he made the rest of us look good.

In theoretical chemistry, though, he was brilliant, and that's what got him through the courses. In the actual experiments he was hopeless. He was forever omitting some critical interim step or ingredient, or mixing the wrong reagents, or worse.

At the end of the semester we had to turn in clean, dry glassware, or else be charged for it. He had a tarred 500 cc round-bottom flask. The routine technique for tar removal is to pour in a solution of dichromate/sulfuric. Let it set overnight. The tar dissolves. The r.b. is bright and clean by next lab session. Kash put some permanganate in his r.b., followed by a nice slug of sulfuric, stoppered the flask, and was going to put it in his cabinet, when it blew. Fortunately it wasn't pointing at anybody. He looked around, grinned sheepishly, washed it out. It was as clean as the day it came from the factory.

Oxygen can be made by heating potassium chlorate catalyzed with a little manganese dioxide in a test tube and leading the gas into a collecting vessel in a pneumatic trough. The gas is fun to play with. You can heat the tip of an iron wire red hot in a Bunsen flame and hold the glowing wire with tongs in the collected oxygen. Lavoisier had done this a hundred and fifty years earlier, and we were supposed to repeat the experiment in general chemistry. It didn't work for Kash. He collected no oxygen. He had forgotten to add the manganese dioxide catalyst.

Hydrogen, one of our most valuable elements, is used for making ammonia, hydrogenating vegetable oils to make Crisco, and so on. We made experimental quantities of hydrogen (and by-product oxygen) by simple electrolysis of water. Faraday had given precise instructions a century earlier. It was the simplest experiment in the lab manual. But Kash got not a single cc of either hydrogen or by-product oxygen. He made several attempts. The first time, he connected the batteries wrong. The next time, he actually did make hydrogen, but he had forgotten to displace the air in his collecting tubes with water, so he couldn't collect anything. In his third attempt everything was just right, but he still got no current flow. He had forgotten to add a pinch of electrolyte.

That's the way it went. In quant, he would forget to get a tare on his porcelain cups before calcining. Or if he remembered that, he would forget to put "K" on his cup lids, and the product would inevitably be lost.

According to rumor Dr. Johannsen, the department head, had had a long talk with Kash, early on, and had pointed out the advantages of various of the liberal arts programs offered by the university, programs involving no chemistry. To no avail. Kash was determined to get that chemical B.S. Despite possible danger to himself and his lab-mates, he considered it his patriotic duty, especially in these troubled times.

In 1938 Hitler and Chamberlain conferred at Munich. Thomas Wolfe died. *Rebecca,* by Daphne du Maurier. *Pygmalion,* a movie with Leslie Howard and Wendy Hiller. And Helen and I were married.

It was a very simple wedding. Her mother drove up from Florida and returned a couple of days later.

My mother came up on the *Tennesseean* and stayed for a couple of days at a tourist hotel across the street from our apartment building. She took only a half-hearted interest in the nuptials. I knew what was bothering her. Mord had resigned from the Seminary faculty. Forced out, according to certain nasty rumors. Mother didn't – *couldn't* – believe what his enemies were whispering about him. She couldn't sleep at night. Bags drooped under her eyes. She had lost weight. The trauma was killing her. Everything she held sacred was going down the drain. I think her main object in coming to Washington in 1938 was to get reassurance from me about Mord. The wedding was just incidental.

We got off together for a few minutes the morning of the ceremony. She lifted pleading eyes to mine. "Joseph, you knew him. It's all a pack of lies, isn't it? But tell me the truth, no matter what."

I took her hand and I looked down into her worn face. "He had enemies, Mother. Some of them, very cruel, very mean. I know what they're saying. It's simply not true, none of it, not a word." I gathered strength. "He preached to boys, in the alleys, in the streets, like St. Francis preaching to the birds. And when a boy was picked up for a petty crime like purse snatching or shoplifting, the police would often let Dr. Mord ride with the boy in the paddy wagon, to let the kid know that he was still a child of God and that Christ loved him, regardless of what he had done. So *of course* the good man was in jail from time to time. That's where he did some of his best preaching. It was his work, his mission, with the boys, and all. I saw him there myself, in the city jail. A touching experience, I might add. Besides the boys, he was baritone with the Friday night Seminary choir. Fine voice. I'll never forget him."

She closed her eyes and took an immense breath.

"I knew it. I'm ashamed that I ever doubted. A great role model for you, Joseph, and for all young men. Oh, thank you, thank you. I can go to my rest in peace."

I seized the opportunity. "And I guess this means you finally forgive me for switching to chemistry?"

She looked up at me with wondering eyes. "Not at all. I'm surprised you ask. Really, Joseph!"

We had no money, so there was no reception. And no honeymoon. I took off four days annual leave, and that was it.

We were very happy.

Helen unpacked the wedding gifts as they came in and wrote the thank-you notes.

One gift gave her trouble. And me. In fact it brought my heart into my throat.

She held it up. She took it out onto our little balcony for a closer examination in better light. She came back in and gave it to me. "What is it?"

By then I had got control of my voice. "Why, an olive dish, I think. Looks like some I've seen at Garfinkels. Who sent it?"

It wasn't an olive dish, and I knew well who had sent it. Cybele had evidently left death-bed instructions with her mother, and as soon as Di had learned that I was getting married, she had prepared and mailed the little package, complete with enclosure, and no return address.

Helen was going through the box, and fingering the wrappings. "No card. Weird. Let's see. Postmarked – well, hard to make out. Yes, Fort West. And the packing wads . . . the *Star-Telegram*. And wait, here's something . . ."

She pulled a sheaf of slips of paper from the box. They were stapled together at the upper left-hand corner. "What in the world . . . ?" She handed them to me.

I considered them gravely. "Very mysterious." What they were, were the forged library slips I had stolen from Cybele's desk at JimBowie years ago. I had thought I was so smart. But I had got away with nothing. The flaw in my otherwise perfect crime was, all passes were routinely returned to the originating teachers. She had known all along. "Maybe somebody will eventually tell us," I said, rather lamely.

So Helen went on to other matters, and I examined the slips further, one by one. The last one had something on it in Cybele's handwriting, a chemical equation. She was evidently trying to tell me something, but for the life of me, I couldn't imagine what.

I put the slips away in a little cedar box on our bureau, and as I closed the lid I noted the faint ethereal odor: bluebonnets, of course.

And that "olive dish." It must have cost her several hundred dollars. It was actually a thick-walled platinum cupel, such as might be used in holding a highly corrosive mixture of something at red-heat. That much

I could understand. She was telling me that, at some time in the future, I would have occasion to use it.

We put it away, behind our ten-dollar set of dinner dishes in our little kitchen cupboard. And there it sat for months, brooding, almost forgotten, quietly waiting.

There wasn't much to our little apartment: just a combination living room and dining room, tiny kitchen, bathroom, bedroom. A miniscule screened porch looked out on a parking lot. We were on the seventh floor; street noises were muted, almost soothing. Our building was within walking distance of work and school.

I accumulated a few chemicals and test tubes in that little kitchen, and once in a while, to Helen's great disgust, I ran some experiments. There was no exhaust fan in the kitchen. I opened the window.

Far below our bedroom window a White Tower carried on a thriving business. On Sundays we went down for hamburgers.

The summer nights were hot. We had a fan, and we raised the windows and hoped for cross breezes. But mostly we just sweltered. We slept fitfully in our underwear. On those nights we could smell the magnolias at the State Department, six blocks away.

Well . . . Along with the "olive dish" I now resolved to put away all thoughts of Cybele. I was married now, and I took my new status very seriously. I wanted to be totally loyal to my dear wife. I tried, I really tried. But things kept coming up. A bar of music . . . a street scene . . . an event in a movie (even though Helen might be sitting next to me). I never mentioned any of this to her, of course.

Did Helen suspect my double mental life? I was never sure. On the other hand it never came out in the open, and I avoided dangerous situations where it might. I think she assumed that before we were engaged I had dated other girls, but I had never given her any details. Sometimes she would look at me in a quirky way, as though she wanted to ask me something, but then apparently decided not to. When I saw trouble coming I would try to lead the discussion into chemistry.

We didn't go to church. For a couple of quasi-reasons. We had no money for the collection plate. And although Helen was a firm Methodist, I was a hopeless pagan. Actually, these were not our real reasons. With my labs and classes nearly every night, Sunday was special for us, our only free day together, with golden hours for catching up on our lovemaking.

Yes, we loved Sundays.

It's Sunday morning, about 7 o'clock. Daylight is streaming in the windows. Helen struggles out of bed, her long dark hair going every which way, and she's yawning and stretching, and scratching the back of her neck. No make-up. I watch this. She is very beautiful. She starts down the hall toward the bathroom. I lie in bed, following her retreating figure with hungry eyes. Her pale blue nightgown flaps around her legs, her buttocks frame curves through the fragile fabric, and I watch, and catch my breath. I am Robert Browning, watching Elizabeth. *O lyric love! Half angel and half bird, and all a wonder and a wild desire!*

A couple of hours later, after a light brunch of toast and tea, and after other things, we lie spooned together nude in the bed. Eventually I will have to get up and start studying for an exam in organic. Eventually . . .

Formic Acid

May 1942. Helen and I were still living in our little apartment in Washington and working for the government. The country had been at war barely five months. My little brother Patrick Dohman Barnes – Peedo – had been drafted and had already qualified for O.C.S. – Officers Candidate School. My draft board was waiting until I graduated from George Washington to see what they would do with me. I wanted to get into the Chemical Warfare Service, but for this I'd need my B.S., which, right now, was way up in the air. I needed one more prep in Advanced Organic Lab. Dr. Nolan had let us choose our own. "But you'll have to finish it by Friday, 10 p.m.," he warned sternly. "At ten sharp all labs close down tight for the semester."

For me, there were other conditions, which he didn't mention. To pass the course, I had to make a B on the prep.

And there was another little matter. To have the necessary semester hours to graduate, I had to pass the course. Everything was tied to this one final prep.

I chose the synthesis of formic acid. Why formic? Well (I told myself), the higher members of the monobasic acids have high boiling points and are odorless, but can't be synthesized by simple in vitro techniques. Acids in the middle range, valeric to capric, have an awful clinging odor. No thanks. Coming on down, there were several clever ways to make butyric and propionic. And I was sorely tempted to make acetic by the catalytic oxidation of acetaldehyde. But no. Something drove me back to the beginning of the series: to formic acid – named for *formix,* the ant, because if you dry distill a few thousand ants (Albert Schweitzer, forgive!), you get formic acid. Ants, bees, wasps sting you with formic acid. But I found that I was thinking mostly of ants, big red ants. I had flashes of forgotten memories. Oh well, on with the prep.

There were several possible synthesis routes. It didn't take me long to zero in on the thermal decomposition of oxalic acid, catalyzed by a little glycerine. First, glycerol oxalate forms; this ester then decomposes to formic ester with loss of CO_2. The formic ester then reacts with more oxalic acid to give formic acid and regenerate the oxalic ester. Formic acid product boils at 101° C, and it should be easy to distill it out in good yield and condense it.

At seven that evening I checked into the lab with springy step. My formic prep shouldn't take more than an hour, ninety minutes at most. I'd get a B. I'd pass. I'd graduate in ten days. They'd take me in Chemical Warfare (motto, "Let Us Rule the Battle by Means of the Elements").

My battle for my chemistry degree had started eight years ago, and now it was over.

Except it wasn't.

Things began to go wrong. To start, the war-time rubber shortage had hit the supply of rubber tubing – an absolute necessity for Bunsen burners and water-cooled condensers, both of which I had to have for my prep. You had to borrow specified lengths from the stock room and leave your punch card as surety for their return. It was ironic. Berzelius had invented the use of rubber tubing in the laboratory, and now there was no rubber to be had: the Japanese navy had cut us off from Indonesia. When I finally got my tubing half an hour later and was setting everything up, I found that the glycerine stock bottle was empty. The stock clerk told me there was a five-gallon carboy in the basement store room, which was locked. And where was the key? There were various ideas.

I walked slowly back to my bench. Was the glycerine absolutely necessary? Of course, simply heating oxalic will give you a *little* HCOOH. But I had to get a yield of at least ten percent. That was the rule. All preps had to make at least ten percent, or they weren't accepted.

I looked at my neighbor at the adjacent bench. Kash had been working on his prep for three weeks. Tonight he was fractionally distilling his product, five liters of crude benzene. He was watching that big r.b. flask, and he was frowning. Occasionally the liquid in the flask would "bump," and a big bubble would surge up into the distilling column. This was all wrong. If an organic liquid is to boil smoothly and productively, you have to add boiling stones: several bits of unglazed porcelain the size of your fingernail. The liquid in contact with the porous surfaces readily vaporizes and makes millions of tiny bubbles which rise to the surface, whence their vapors pass on into the distilling column. With boiling stones distillation proceeds smoothly, but the stones have to be added at the beginning. You should never add them to the hot liquid. Repeat, *never.*

Kash had forgotten to add his boiling stones. He'd have to dismantle everything, chill his benzene in an ice bath, and start over. And maybe not finish in time. Tough. I knew exactly how he felt.

I watched him stride grimly over to the reagent bench and unscrew the lid from the jar of chips.

I wasn't paying much attention. Glycerine, I thought. Once long long ago in Fort West I had bought a little bottle from the drugstore. I had made (maybe) nitroglycerine. Now, there was a drugstore on G Street, just across from the lab building. In this synthesis glycerine is a catalyst. I don't need much. An ounce should do. Out and back in fifteen minutes. Maybe ten. I can do it. I turned and started for the doors.

And just then I had another thought. My hapless neighbor and his boiling stones. He had returned to his bench and he was holding a 250-cc beaker half-full of stones. It was quite clear he wasn't going to bother chilling his flask. He was going to dump those chips straight into that super-heated benzene. I heard some one cry out, "No! No! Stop him!" I called out a warning. "Kash!" Then that urgent voice again. *"Joe, run for the door!"*

I turned and ran.

There was a tremendous prolonged WHOOMP and a prolonged yellow flash behind me. I rose gracefully into the air. The swinging doors opened magically ahead of me. I sailed through them and out into the hall.

And while I was in the air I understood why I had been both attracted and repelled by formic acid. It came to me in a series of nearly instantaneous flashes, the way they say your whole life flashes before you when you think you're about to die.

I am floating majestically through those lab doors, and I am simultaneously back at Riverside, our home in Colorado City, Texas, before we moved to Fort West. I am six or seven years old. Mother asked me to take a pan of laundry out to the clothes lines in the back yard. I did. Coming back, I put the basin on top of a nest of red ants (big mean fellows, easily three-quarters of an inch long). One of them had stung me once, and I hated them.

I got in the basin. The sides were too slick for the ants to crawl up, and I could study them in safety. I did this every time I went out to hang clothes on the lines. After a time, I'd tire of ant-inspection and return the basin to the back porch.

On this particular occasion my little brother Peedo picked up the basin and lugged it with much effort and clatter down to the ant nest. I watched this from the kitchen window. I was not particularly alarmed. Peedo lived in a world of his own. I sensed vaguely that he was trying to imitate my forays into the world of *formix*. As I watched, he put the pan down on the approximate center of the nest. Then he tried to get in it, but the sides were high, and he was having trouble.

I suspected then that something bad was about to happen. I was right.

Peedo began to scream. Then he sat down. Aunt Molly, our cleaning lady, threw her broom down, ran outside, grabbed him, brushed ants off his flesh and clothing, and rushed back onto the porch, where she peeled him and began dosing his skin with bluing, the rural remedy for insect bites. Poor little Patrick calmed down to an intermittent whimper. Whether it was the bluing or Aunt Molly's cuddling, nobody cared. And actually, there's a sound chemical basis for the efficacy of this laundry adjunct. Bluing is an aqueous solution of ferric ferricyanide, which can destroy formic acid, $HCOOH$, by oxidizing it to H_2O and CO_2.

I had forgotten the ants until now. They had lain dormant under tons of guilt. I had set a lousy example for my little brother. And when I should have rushed out and pulled him away, I had just stood there, paralyzed.

"Barnes? Joe?" Voices were calling to me.

"He's coming around," somebody said.

I was on my back, looking up at familiar faces.

"How do you feel?" Professor Nolan asked.

"Okay, I think." They helped me get to my feet. "I'm okay," I repeated. I looked down at my pants legs. They were ripped out. My hands and knees were bleeding. "Kash?" I groaned.

"Bad burns," somebody said. "Ambulance coming."

It was pretty clear what had happened. When Kash tossed those little bits of crockery into his five liters of hot benzene, it vaporized instantly. That's a lot of hot vapor. And then the vapor ignited, and made more hot vapor, *lots* more. *That's* what blew me out of the doors. And since benzene makes a lot of soot when it burns, a black cloud settled over everything.

We stood aside in silent fear as the stretchermen carried Kash out. He had no face.

After the ambulance and firemen left, Dr. Nolan called us all back into the shambles of the lab.

Nothing was left at my bench. My poor prep, I thought. I don't graduate.

But Nolan was both philosophical and merciful. He checked us off, one by one. He said to me, "You had a prep?"

I felt a sudden hope. I described it. He listened carefully as I went through the steps.

"Total wipe-out?" he said.

"Yes sir."

"I'll give you an A."

He handed out four A's. One chap who hadn't even started got a B.

On the way back to the apartment that night I was thinking all sorts of mixed-up thoughts. How to hide from Helen the rips in my britches and the lacerations in my hands and knees. And ole Peedo, now somewhere in North Carolina. He'd be going – where? England? The Pacific? God protect you, Peedo, and I hope you do a better job than I did so long ago!

And overlying all these thoughts there was something else. Back there at the bench, just before the big blow, I had heard a woman shouting at me. There had been no woman in the lab, and yet I had heard a woman cry out to me, *"Joe! Run for the door!"* I knew that voice. Cybele, of course. She had intervened. She may have saved my life. Thank you, my darling, for me, for Helen.

Graduation ceremonies were held on June 7, 1942, in Constitution Hall. It was just a couple of blocks from where we lived, and Helen and I walked down.

On the Hall corner a boy was selling extras of the *Star*. According to the headlines a great sea and air battle had been fought the day before near the island of Midway, and four Japanese aircraft carriers had been sunk. Marvelous! Maybe a few less bullets headed toward Peedo.

So what happened after graduation? I didn't go into Chemical Warfare. The Bureau of Mines vetoed my request for transfer. It was probably just as well.

Law School

Here's why I entered law school.

By June 1942, when I walked down that aisle at Constitution Hall and Dr. Cloyd Heck Marvin handed me my B.S. diploma, I had already figured it out. Helen worked. I wanted to retire her. For this I needed to make more money.

Nearly every Sunday I went down to the newsstand on Pennsylvania Avenue and got the *Star* and studied the want ads. Washington was teeming with lawyers. Every government department, every agency, had its own legal section. In the ads, lawyers were offered as much money as chemical Ph.D.'s. Law school was four years at night. A Ph.D. would need eight or ten. I had already put in eight, just for my B.S. I couldn't handle another eight.

And it was time I faced up to my limitations. I had studied those stalwarts – from Lavoisier to Curie – and I knew they were way out of my league. They had something I didn't, and I didn't know exactly what it was. *They* had done all the necessary groundwork, they had laid down the principles. It's not as wonderful as it once was.

Oh Cybele, how can I explain bitter economic necessity to you? Right now, today, to leave my desk in the Bureau and go into entry- level bench work in any chemical lab in or out of government would mean taking a serious cut in pay. No.

Interesting dilemma. If I stay in chemistry, I'm disloyal to Helen; if I leave chemistry I'm disloyal to Cybele. Well, at least for the time being, I'm faithful to both. Barely. In the Bureau, I'm still a P-3 chemist, but in four years I'll be something different. Not sure what. A chemist with a law degree? A lawyer with a B.S. in chemistry? Maybe I'll know, when the time comes.

Cybele, are you out there, watching all this? Are you, like the ghost of Hamlet's father, doomed for a time to walk the earth? Do you want to be released? Do you want *not* to be released? What do *I* want for you? I don't know. I can't keep you, I can't let you go. What do you think about my going into law? Do you forgive me? On the day I take the bar, will you disappear? Questions, questions. No answers.

Barite

On this occasion in 1944 I was inventorying the country's supply of barite – barium sulfate. (The miners called it "barytes" and pronounced it "bear-tease." They stared at you if you called it by its dictionary name.) By whatever name, this odd heavy white mineral, $BaSO_4$, was absolutely essential in drilling wells in high-pressure oil fields. The driller fed it into the well as "drilling mud," and it did various nice things such as preventing the drill rig from being blown out of the hole, lubricating the drill bit, floating the cuttings up and out of the well, and so on.

Half a billion years ago, when these Tennessee mountains were simply immense layers of mud collecting at the bottom of a great inland sea, clusters of barium ions were floating around in those murky waters and knocking into other ions. And whenever they hit sulfate ions, they precipitated, forming misshapen white masses, which, depending on the continuing availability of feed ions, might stretch as flattened columns a hundred yards or more. And then they would settle. And then, over a few hundred million more years, the seabottom would rise, as though to see what the dinosaurs were doing, and then the new plateau would age, and wrinkle, and the ribbons of barite would shatter, and all you'd see would be pieces, fist size, toe size, a few head size, hidden away in marl or limestone like raisins in pudding.

Came the twentieth century. The limestone had turned to raw dirt. The trick now was to collect the pieces of barite and sell them. Clever men in Georgia and Tennessee and Missouri brought in diesel shovels and loaded the mix of white lumps and black dirt onto trucks, and dumped the loads into washers, where the dirt was washed away and the barite was left, for collection and shipment.

I was in Boone, a little town in Tennessee, near Oak Ridge. I finished my report for Tennessee and put it in the mail. It would get bounced around in Washington. Mines would send it to War Manpower, where the numbers of barite miners needed in Tennessee would be measured against requirements for draftees, policemen, scientists, and so on. A copy could go to the War Production Board. Now nobody could order a local draft board to defer anybody, but explanations could be made, like, "no barite, no oil." And everybody remembered how, in that other war, the British had drafted young Henry Moseley, their most brilliant scientist, and stupidly got him killed at Gallipoli.

This time around the British were more careful, and we were trying to do likewise. It was a new kind of war, and American draft boards were cautious.

A lot of people who lived in Boone actually worked in Oak Ridge, and apparently in three shifts. The bus leaving Boone at six in the morning would pass the bus from Oak Ridge dragging home the dog-tired midnight shift. Funny thing was, you couldn't find Oak Ridge on any map of Tennessee; yet everybody knew that something tremendous was going on there. But what, nobody seemed to know. Whatever it was, it tied up transportation, housing, phones, laundry – everything – for miles around. And therein lay my problem: I had to get to the Missouri barite fields, near St. Louis, where I could talk to the major producers in the area. Trains were a big question. In the coaches it was standing room only. Could I stand in a crowded swaying aisle for eight hours? Maybe I'd have to. I groaned. I'd be in sad shape for conferences the next day. I knew I couldn't get a Pullman to St. Louis, but I knew I had to try.

The little hotel was two blocks from the B & O station. I walked into the station and approached the ticket window.

There were three people in line ahead of me. One by one they asked for a Pullman berth to St. Louis, and one by one they were turned away.

My turn came. I stepped up. Why am I wasting time here, I thought.

The agent and I looked at each other. I'll never forget the sad eyes under the cracked green visor. He got ready to shake his head. But then a long freight started through. We couldn't talk. We could both see this was going to take a while. And while I was thinking, I wondered . . . I sniffed. Yes. Bluebonnets.

He picked up the phone. I hadn't heard it. He looked up at me. His lips formed the words. "St. Louis?"

I nodded. There had been a cancellation. I was at the right place at exactly the right time. He wrote it up. A lower berth, for heaven's sake!

I looked past him into his grimy paint-flaking office. Motion? A skirt? Someone had disappeared into an inner doorway.

A couple of hours later I was on the train. I got a Coke in the club car while the porter made up my berth, and then I turned in.

A hop and a skip over the next ridge, about forty miles northeast of Chattanooga, at the foot of the Cumberland escarpment, and we sped through the little town of Dayton.

Now most Texans would feel right at home in Tennessee. In fact, Tennessee is known as the Volunteer State, because of the large numbers of Tennesseeans who volunteered in the Mexican War. A lot of them stayed in Texas after the war was over.

The Tennessee legislature has passed some fine legislation, which would have been heartily approved by many in the Lone Star State. Take the Tennessee law that *pi* was 3 exactly. None of this complicated silly stuff about 3.1416. No, they simplified it right off, to the eternal gratitude of future millions of school kids. Another law, much better known, was, nobody in a state-supported school could teach that "man is descended from the lower animals."

Which brings us back to Dayton. In July 1925 John T. Scopes, a Dayton high school biology teacher, taught that man evolved from an ape-like ancestor. He was arrested, tried, and despite a blistering defense by

Clarence Darrow, found guilty and fined one hundred dollars. William Jennings Bryan was a star witness for the prosecution.

I greatly admired Bryan. A large part of my admiration was perhaps a bit askew. It was based on the fact that a brilliant, educated man, who once had run for president, was able to force half of his mind to believe that the world had been created only six thousand years ago, and that our first ancestors were Adam (with a rib missing) and Eve, while the other half of his mind could not only understand the intricate economics of gold and silver, but was also able to explain it to the common folk. He was simultaneously a Fundamentalist and a realist. And that earned my awe, respect, and admiration.

I had taken a couple of law books with me on the trip. Propped up on two pillows in my opulent lower berth I studied Conflict and Taxation.

When we stopped for a time in Nashville I began to yawn, and as we pulled out I drifted away, lulled by the rhythmic metallic melody of the wheels:

Cy-be-le, Cy-be-le, Cy-be-le. . . .

The Conversion

Every three months my draft board yielded to the entreaties of the Undersecretary of the Interior Department and notified me that my deferment was being continued.

This was silly. My little brother Peedo was already through OCS and was headed for Germany. I was going to be left out. ("What did you do in the war, Daddy?")

I wrote my draft board. What I was doing, I said, could be done by an older man, or by a woman. A degree in chemistry was useful but not really necessary. They listened. They canceled my deferment. They gave me a date to report for my physical. I alerted my boss, Dr. Schaefer. I was on my way. Well, not quite. Dr. Schaefer called Mr. Andros, the Undersecretary, who called the chairman of my draft board. The deferment was back on. Dr. Schaefer invited me into his office. He looked calm, but actually I could see that he was seething. His face was white, with red spots. I was scared. There was a brief discussion, mostly dealing with my inability to comprehend the nature of modern warfare, and the need for accurate, up-to-date information in mineral requirements. Then he played his trump card. "All right, go on into the military, if that's what you want. As a buck private. But note well, young man, the Secretary has placed a pre-emptive transfer on you with the War Department. The day you're sworn into the army the M.P.s will bring you right back here – as Private Joseph Barnes – at your same desk – at thirty dollars a month. You won't even get a housing allowance."

He waited for me to digest that. It didn't take long. Thirty dollars wouldn't even pay the rent of our little rent-controlled apartment.

The Bureau chief clenched his jaw in hard horizontal lines. "So, are you with us, or not?"

I'm not stupid. "I'm with you."

At this point in my career, if I stayed in the Bureau I was due for an in-grade promotion. But timing was within the chief's discretion, and just now he was very, very disappointed in me. So, in effect, as I left Dr. Schaefer's office, my hoped-for promotion sailed blithely out ahead of me. Or so I thought.

Actually, it was probably just as well that the army wouldn't have me. I would have made a lousy soldier, a danger to myself and the whole platoon.

In 1944 the Pentagon was still under construction. Much of the business of the war was conducted in a series of wooden prefabs spaced along the Mall, left over from World War I. Since they were only "temporary," they were called Tempos.

The War Production Board – the WPB – mostly occupied Tempo E, and included the office of Mr. Nicholas Button, Chief, Non-metallic Minerals.

Today Button and I were on the phone; discussing strontium.

When a machine gun is shooting, particularly at a moving target, such as an airplane, accuracy is improved with tracer bullets. Every fifth bullet carries a charge of flaming color and shows where the bullet spray is going. For example, green from barium, yellow from sodium, and so on. Strontium gives a brilliant red, and both sides used a lot of it.

Strontium comes from a mineral, strontianite, $SrCO_3$, which, although not rare, isn't plentiful either. It's easily processed. Just react it with nitric acid. CO bubbles off, and you get the nitrate, $Sr(NO_3)_2$. By the third year of the war, the Defense Department reported that reserves of strontianite were running low.

That's when Nick Button called me. I knew what he wanted before he really began. We had already looked. We couldn't find any more strontianite for him. What we did find was low-grade celestite – the sulfate, $SrSO_4$, on Strontian Island in Lake Erie and in Blair County, Pennsylvania, and a couple of other places.

He said he would discuss it with his experts and call back. They told him no. It's insoluble. You can't react it with nitric acid. All very true. But so what? I asked him. Why do you need strontium? You've got loads of sodium nitrate. It gives a brilliant yellow trace. "I know," he said, "and we'll use it. The problem is, say six of our guys are shooting at the same Zero, and all the tracers are yellow. It's all mixed up, and they can't tell who's shooting where. We need different colors."

"Okay. Have you tried reacting the sulfate with soda ash? The equilibrium goes to the right, and you get the carbonate."

"Soda ash? No, it's all allocated for the next six months. Right down to the ounce."

"For God's sake, Nick, just a few hundred pounds for the pilot plant? Make a little less soap, a few less Coke bottles? In '38 it was coming out our ears."

"That was *then*. You realize today we're even pumping it out of soda brines in dry lakes in California?"

"Yeah." Sure, I knew that. Trona. I was thinking. I was visualizing reactions. One kept coming back to me.

$$SrSO_4 + 4C \rightarrow SrS + 4CO.$$

I was certain the sulfide was soluble. "How about carbon?" I said.

"What do you mean, carbon?"

"Charcoal, coal, coke . . . it can be most anything. Have to be able to get it into powder form."

"Wait a minute. Coal dust? Lots of coal dust. They flush it into the rivers in West Virginia. Raises hell with the water downstream."

It was a challenge. I was finishing up the spring semester in law school at George Washington – at night, of course, and working seven days a week at the Bureau of Mines and I didn't have a lot of spare time. But I thought of Peedo, and Germans shooting at him, and I got to thinking. I can do it. In fact it's easy. "Powdered celestite and powdered carbon," I said. "Ought to work. I can try it out tonight. I'll call you at home."

"Call me here."

I left the office at five o'clock, and on my way home I picked up a little packet of powdered charcoal from the drugstore. Back in the apartment I extracted the beautiful little crystal of celestite from my mineral collection (*c'est la guerre*), and I took it out on the little porch, wrapped it in heavy cloth, and pounded it to smithereens with a hammer. I mixed the powdered mineral and the powdered carbon with a little spoon, and put the mixture in Cybele's $400 platinum cupel, which up to then had lain empty in our kitchen cupboard. I attached my Bunsen burner to the pilot of the gas stove, stuck the cupel in a ceramic triangle, and put the flame under it. As an afterthought, I opened the window. After all, if it worked, I'd be making a fair amount of carbon monoxide.

I cut law class that evening, of course.

Helen came in from work a few minutes later. She frowned and sniffed and snorted. She didn't approve of using her kitchen as a lab. "Just what are you doing this time?"

"I am converting a low-grade ore."

"A . . . what kind of whore?"

"No. *Ore.*" I explained the project, and she felt better about it. She fixed us some sandwiches. We ate and we watched the little vessel cast up its fumes. After half an hour nothing more seemed to be happening. I scraped out some of the crusty black solids from the container and put a pinch in a test tube with a little water and shook it up. Nice odor of H_2S. Let's filter a few cc. Good clear liquid. Now add a pinch of Na_2CO_3. Fine precip of $SrCO_3$. It worked.

It was 8 o'clock. I called Nick Button at Tempo E and gave him the results. He seemed satisfied, and said he would pass my report along to his several supervisors. I never heard about it again. Maybe it was actually tested somewhere. Maybe it got lost in the wartime bureaucratic shuffle. Maybe it was turned down. Whatever happened or didn't happened was all top secret.

Alleged top secret.

Nobody had told Helen it was secret. A clerk in her office happened to be in my ConLaw class at G.W. I was borrowing his notes for the class I missed, and he asked me (looking around furtively), "Joe, is it true? What's this we hear about converting a low-grade whore?"

I got it instantly. "Well, I certainly tried," I said quietly. "For the rest, we wait, and pray, and hope. You know how these things go."

"Oh. Sure, Joe. Didn't realize you were the religious type."

It wasn't over. Though I didn't know it at the time, reports of my Sr project filtered back into my personnel records at Mines . . . in mangled form.

Dr. Schaefer called me into his office. As I shut the door behind me I noted that he was closing a pink folder on his desk. My personnel file. What awful crime had I committed lately? I couldn't think of any. He motioned to the chair, and I sat, and waited.

He cleared his throat a couple of times. "You'll be interested to know that the WPB is following several of your recommendations in the non-metallic area."

"Oh?"

"They have allocated lead, for its use in tetra-ethyl lead, for gasoline. No surprise there, but your memo on bromine was an eye opener. We must have an equivalent amount of bromine, for the synthesis of ethylene dibromide, for . . ." He fumbled with his notes.

"To prevent lead dioxide fouling of the spark plugs," I offered.

"Ah, yes. That. And then your estimates of magnesium oxide for open-hearth refractories. Not to mention graphite, mica, and asbestos." He pulled a paper from the stack on his desk. "And iodine, needed in photography, medicine, and so on. Left over from Chile nitrate, poorly packed, you say, needs vapor-tight containers. They're looking into that. A little problem, though, Barnes. You've defined iodine vapor losses in terms of e to the minus kt. Perhaps if you converted that to a simpler mathematical expression?"

"Of course, sir."

"And now boron, needed for eye treatment, soap powders, glass. Nice breakdown."

But not a word about strontium, the one thing I'd like to be remembered for.

He'd had all this for weeks. This wasn't why he'd called me in. Was he still rankling about my draft fiasco? That was ages ago. Was he finally going to fire me? In the Washington way, with a sincere farewell pat on the back? I might as well go drown myself. I thought of that black joke about the man drowning in the Potomac. A man rushed down to the shore. "Help me!" cried the drowning man. The newcomer shouted back: "Where do you live?" That summed up the housing situation in wartime Washington.

Dr. Schaefer leaned over his desk and studied me in a curious, almost embarrassed way. Surely not a twinge of conscience, I thought. Let's do it quick and surgical.

He cleared his throat again, and he began. "Sometimes we work together for months, even years, without really knowing . . . understanding . . . and then we suddenly discover . . ." He sighed. "I guess I'm not making any sense. I'm a deacon in the Methodist church. What denomination are you, Barnes?"

I stared at him. What the hell was going on? "I was baptized in the Disciples of Christ . . ." Oh, I well remember. The preacher really dunked me. I thought I was a goner.

"And you studied for the ministry at the seminary in Fort West?"

Very mysterious. "Yes, sir."

"Fine people, the Disciples."

"Yes, sir."

"Yes," he said softly, "we reach out to our fellow man in all walks of life, men, women, especially the poor fallen souls." He stood up and so did I and he came around his desk and we shook hands. "Thank you, Barnes."

I was being dismissed, and I had no idea why I was there in the first place. I walked out in a daze.

My next paycheck was a nice surprise. I had been promoted. And it was three months retroactive. We put the extra money in war bonds.

That evening Helen and I had supper at the S & W. I kept thinking, "Poor fallen souls?" It finally hit me as I was chopping away at my miniscule hamburger patty. I burst out laughing, and people in adjoining tables – not to mention Helen – probably thought I was crazy. Which was okay in Washington during the war.

"Gold! Gold!"

The war was recently over and I was beginning my last year in law school. I was sitting in my little office in the Bureau and wondering about my future. My phone rang. "Mr. Barnes, can you come in here for a moment?" It was the chief, Dr. Schaefer.

As I entered his office a visitor rose from a chair near Schaefer's desk and smiled at me.

The chief said, "Mr. Barnes, have you met Mr. Andros?" I stammered something. We shook hands.

Mr. Andros was the Undersecretary. He was the chap Harold Ickes sent over to take the guff at congressional budget hearings. He ran the Department when Ickes was away, which was most of the time. He was the man who had scotched my attempt to get myself drafted. So *now* what awful crime had I committed?

Maybe none. They were both smiling at me. But in Washington, D.C., that didn't mean anything.

Dr. Schaefer's smile relaxed. He got to the point. "Mr. Barnes, is there any gold in sea water?"

I thought, O God, not Sarah Winters again! "Yes, sir."

"How much?"

I frowned, and tried to recall something I had read. Yes. Frank Wigglesworth Clarke's famous *Data of Geochemistry.* "Analyses vary, sir. The average seems to be about four micrograms of gold per metric ton of seawater. However, values as high as 60 micrograms have been reported. Of course, even that's not a lot. On the other hand, terrestrial deposits are being worked commercially today where the Au concentration is less than that. And of course, the aggregate amount of gold in seawater is enormous."

"How much?" asked Andros.

"It has been estimated at ten billion metric tons."

Andros whistled softly. "So why hasn't somebody tried to recover it?"

"Oh, they have, sir. There have been dozens of serious attempts."

"Indeed?"

"Yes sir. For example, in the 1870s, after the Franco-Prussian War, the French tried hard to recover gold from seawater to help pay off Bismark's war indemnity. They recovered a bit of gold, but they found the process cost more than the value of the gold they recovered. The Germans made a similar effort in the twenties, to pay war reparations. Their chief chemist, Fritz Haber, worked out a process, and they actually equipped a ship and sent it out, but nothing came of the project."

"How did they go about it?" asked Andros. "Do we know anything about the processes?" Both of them watched me expectantly.

"It's all pretty well known. All those efforts involved precipitating gold as the highly insoluble hydroxide, or as an insoluble salt, such as the iodide or sulfide. The big trouble was, you had to get rid of a bunch of other stuff – sodium, calcium, magnesium, and so on, before you could even think about bringing down the Au. They tried electrolysis, dialysis, chromatography."

"So?" said Andros. "Go on."

"Well, sir, it was good, it was bad. It was tantalizing. The good part was, everything worked. They got gold, generally as microscopic flakes. The bad thing was, the process always cost more to run than the market value of the gold it produced."

"What was the main expense?" asked Dr. Schaefer.

"The volume of seawater."

"I guess they had to move a lot," Andros said.

I did some quick mental arithmetic. "Yes sir. If you give it the most optimistic extreme, say the feed analyzes 60 milligrams per metric ton, then to recover one ounce, we're talking something of the order of 20 billion gallons of seawater, and big, big corrosion-resistant pumps. Stainless steel is expensive."

"Yes, stainless steel pumps," said Andros. "I've seen estimates. They'd come by boat, from Siemens, in Germany. Our contact has been working on this for ten years. He claims he finally has the answer. He says the refining, fully amortized, costs $18 per ounce of gold, currently selling at $30." He pulled a little leather pouch from his jacket pocket and handed it to me. "Is that gold?"

I loosed the drawstring and looked inside. The pouch was heavy. But lots of metals are heavy. The powder was a dark brown. I knew gold dust could take on a variety of colors, black, purple, blue, pink. It doesn't have to glitter. I shrugged. "It could very well be. Only a chemical analysis could say for sure." I handed it back.

Andros said, "I'm told it's been analyzed as 90 percent pure."

"And the rest?"

"Mostly silver, copper, and platinum."

I thought about that. The analysis was typical and routine. But something was wrong. I couldn't put my finger on it. I suddenly decided I wanted out. We were headed for another Sarah Winters. Somebody was in serious trouble. Me? I looked over at Dr. Schaefer and raised my eyebrows. He understood what I was asking: What's the point of all this? Why am I here?

"We," he said guardedly, "are looking at a new process."

I thought quickly. That could mean most anything. Who is "we"? And what did he mean, "new"? Well, he had opened the game with pawn to queen four, and it was now my turn. The clock was running, and I had to play. Keep it non-committal for the opening moves. I said, "I would assume the process in question utilizes several features not available to the prior investigators? Ion exchange resins, chelates, the ultracentrifuge?" Your move, Andros.

He looked at me curiously. "As a matter of fact, all that's in the flowsheet."

"You've met the inventor?"

"Yes." His eyes bored hard into mine. He suddenly looked grim. "I know you haven't seen the flowsheet. I can't give you you any details. But . . . just from what you've heard, what do you think? Anything – *obviously* wrong?"

I swallowed hard. I could guess what was going on. And it was the worst possible scenario. A relative of somebody way up in government wanted the Bureau to endorse a gold-from-seawater scheme. Maybe even the White House was involved. Damned if you do, damned if you don't.

The situation was loaded with black comedy. I couldn't ask for details of their secret process. All I had to do was tell them whether or not it was any good.

I looked over at Dr. Schaefer. He was perspiring faintly. I could see he wanted to press a handkerchief against his brow, but that he was afraid to move.

And just then I realized what was wrong with this new process. Andros's analysis was for gold taken out of the ground. It had the wrong impurities for gold precipitated from seawater.

The realization did not help. Things just got scarier.

Should I tell the Undersecretary he was embroiled in a fraud? In fact, *was* it a fraud? Did these few grains condemn the whole process? So what should I do?

I thought about how Genghis Khan dealt with messengers bearing bad news. He simply killed them. Definitive.

Deep inside I moaned. Oh, Cybele! And just then I experienced a remarkable auditory phenomenon. I heard (*thought* I heard?) Cybele's voice. "Gold! Gold!" she was croaking harshly.

The two men were staring at me oddly. I held up a finger, motioning for silence. I thought back, back . . . Cybele disappeared. I thought of the Police Department darkroom, the chemicals, the hypo, the acetic acid bath. The smells. Pieces of the puzzle were beginning to assemble. Just a question of putting them together. It was something that happened long ago, even before my tour of duty in the Police Department. Think *back,* Joe! *Way* back!

Yes, Cybele again. JimBowie High, that Hallowe'en party, at the end of October, in the school cafeteria. As her star pupil, I was privileged to help her set up her things on one of the lunch tables. She wore a witch costume, with black skirt and tall conical hat. Probably made them herself. The lights went down. She explained the meaning of Hallowe'en. It was the night before All Hallows Day, and witches and demons were abroad . . . so watch out! At that she swished her skirts, leered out into her enthralled audience, took a sip of water, and spit it out onto the table, where it burst into a dozen spurts of purple flame. Gasps and shrieks from both students and chaperoning faculty. One of the older female teachers whispered, "See? Didn't I tell you? She really *is* a witch."

Actually, she had merely repeated a routine bit of chemical magic. It wasn't water she had taken a sip of. It was plain old alcohol. She had spurted it onto scattered pieces of chromic oxide, a strong oxidizing agent lying unnoticed on the table, and the oxidant had instantly ignited the alcohol. The trick is to get the alcohol in and out of your mouth quickly, before it blisters your tongue.

But that was just the curtain raiser, to sort of get their attention. That, it did.

On with her demonstration.

She leaned over her table. "On this night," she said in a harsh conspiratorial whisper, "we witches can find gold. Most anywhere." She waved her wand over a jar of water. Instantly the liquid turned a sparkling yellow. "Gold!" she cawed. "Gold! Gold!" More gasps. I knew this one, too. I knew how she had done it.

The last I remember of that scene was her eyes. They locked briefly with mine. And I could see how the JimBowie faculty might think she was a witch. She wouldn't have lasted ten minutes in Colonial Salem.

One more thing. Sitting there with Andros and Dr. Schaefer, I was thinking, running my eye – or rather, nose – down a mental list. Bluebonnets – Cybele, of course. Not diagnostically applicable here. Next, fruity smells on breath – diabetes. Plucked feathers – German measles. Stale beer – scrofula. Baking bread – typhoid. Butcher's shop – yellow fever. Ah.

None of the above. But now I knew what questions to ask. Andros broke in impatiently. "Well?"

I faced my executioners. I began slowly. "Mr. Andros . . . when you first met your inventor, did you have occasion to smell his breath?"

They both looked at me blankly, then at each other, then back to me. "You mean, had he been drinking?" snapped Andros. "What kind of silly question is that?"

"It's not a silly question, Mr. Andros. Did his breath smell like garlic? Please answer."

His eyes widened. His mouth opened and closed. "Why, yes, I think it did. Why do you ask? What's the significance?"

"Did he demonstrate the process for you?"

"Well, yes. Just on a very small scale, with little jars."

"And the demonstration liquids had an odor? Like rotten eggs?"

They both stared at me in the dead silence.

I said, "I take that as 'yes.' And finally, your chap is an amateur photographer? Has his own darkroom?" Andros's face gave me the answer. A hit, a very palpable hit.

"Young man," he said sternly, "I think you'd better explain." The way he said it, I was guilty of something very serious.

Okay, Andros, I thought. Let's see if you can take it. "You need two solutions. You make them up with chemicals you can get at the corner drugstore. One solution is 1 gram sodium arsenite in 50 cc of water, with

5 or 6 cc glacial acetic acid. The other solution is 10 grams of photographer's hypo in 50 cc water. Mix the two solutions, and after about 30 seconds you get a beautiful 'gold' precipitate – which is actually simply arsenious sulfide. Hydrogen sulfide – essence of rotten eggs – is released during the process." All exactly the way Cybele had done it that Halloween night so long ago.

"How about the garlic breath?" asked Dr. Schaefer.

"Sure sign of arsenic poisoning, sir." I looked at them both in turn. "Your inventor, Mr. Andros, has been soaking up arsenic for several years, and now it's killing him. Not to mention that H_2S itself is highly toxic. If you want to do him a big favor, get him to a doctor. You might save his life. Sir."

Mr. Andros studied the ceiling a moment. As he rose to leave, he smiled. "No, let him die."

Washington, D.C.

Sarah Winters, are you laughing?

They dismissed me. For the time being.

Next morning, Dr. Schaefer phoned me. Andros wanted to see me in his office. *Now* what?

"I understand you have just finished law school?"

"Yes sir."

"D.C. bar?"

"Next week."

"Any plans?"

"Nothing definite." Ah. I had it. I knew why I was here. Interior was charged with the duty of compiling the famous Strategic Materials list: metals, non-metals, asbestos to uranium, how much of what, where to get it, how and where to store it, how much would it cost. These materials would be bought and stockpiled, ready for World War III. At the moment the only career in government that really interested me was in the Strategic Materials Section.

Andros was the ringmaster for the SM circus. I knew it employed six lawyers, all at two or three P levels higher than me. Evidently all six had blown the big gold scam. He was looking around.

He stood. The interview was over. "Thank you for coming, Barnes." Translation: "Maybe I'll have a vacancy, maybe I won't. Maybe you should call me if you pass the bar. And maybe the incoming administration will cancel the whole thing, and we'll all be out of jobs."

The Washington *maybe* – implied or expressed – covers all possibilities, all eventualities, past, present, future. It requires no explanation, no apology.

"Thank you, sir." I nodded and left.

Mary Ellen Barnes

Helen is due any day now, almost any hour. A good time, a bad time. It will probably coincide with the D.C. Bar Exam.

1945, last year. She was twenty-eight, and her biological clock was running. Faster, faster . . . You didn't need a stethoscope to hear it. You could put your ear on her chest, and there it was, a loud tick-tock, tick-tock, and sometimes tock-tick. It was like listening to Spike Jones's orchestra adrift on a river of estrogen.

We wanted a girl. We talked about names. In Texas all girls have two names, like Mary Louise, Lulu Belle, Nancy Lee, Daisy Nell, and so on. (Yes, Helen actually had two names: Alice Helen. But she didn't like Alice.) Two names for girls was one of the unwritten Texas laws, like in France, where (I am told) by written law all children have to be named after saints. So we agreed on Mary Ellen.

We decided to conceive Mary Ellen one dark December evening in 1945. The exactly right egg lay waiting. The war had been over for four months. I had one more semester of law school at George Washington University, and I was already deeply involved in Mr. Nacrelli's bar review course downtown. The time was ripe.

We met after work and had supper at the S & W, then, holding hands, we walked back in the dark, past the White House to the Churchill Arms, where we lived. Winter darkness in Washington was peculiar. Street lamps centered vague luminous spheres. Tonight everything was very beautiful, especially Helen. I looked at her, and I thought of Byron's poem: 'She walks in beauty, like the night . . .' "

We went inside, checked our mail (nothing), and Bill the elevator boy took us on up to the seventh floor.

Does a woman know the instant, the fact, of conception, when that irresistible little tadpole crashes the egg's protective shell? Some claim they know. Maybe Helen did. I do remember the wonderful smile on her face that night as she slept.

A few weeks later she called me at the office. She is indeed pregnant. Due the middle of September. The embryo is already two months old. Well, Missy, how you have grown! I have read the books. We assume she'll be a girl, but of course we'll be happy with whatever we get. At one month you were smaller than a pea, with fish gills and tiny buds that were growing into arms and legs. At 42 days bone formed, you acquired fingers and toes, a tiny tail (soon to vanish). Right now your body is so water soaked it's transparent. At 46 days your sex organs appeared. Grotesque face. Your umbilical cord works. By now all the evolutionary changes necessary to call you a human being have been accomplished. No longer an embryo. At two months you're a real genuine fetus, almost two inches long!

Later. At three months our daughter is beginning to move. She "breathes" her amniotic fluid in and out of tiny lungs. She can swallow. She makes urine; Helen removes it in her own kidneys. Her bones are funny. They grow by starting in the middle, growing outward, and meeting at the joints. She now has all her organs, but if she were taken from Helen's womb, she would die.

Five months. She kicks a lot, but she also sleeps a lot. Helen tries to synchronize with her, get a little rest. The little eyes are sensitive to light, but of course she can't really see. No hearing yet. Ribs, blood vessels visible through her translucent skin. About the size of my fist. Helen pours the calcium to her. Growing like a weed, but still can't survive outside her mother.

Six months, twelve inches long, about 1-1/2 pounds. Last night she had hiccups. Poor Helen. Loose wrinkled skin, like an old crone. From here on in she just grows. We wait. It won't be long now.

Cybele, are you still out there, or have we now come to a parting of the ways? And if you *are* out there, *where* is "out there"? The Catholics recognize limbo, or "limbus" – a place in between heaven and hell. Neutral. A sort of vacuum. Apparently it was first mentioned in Dante's *Inferno*. Is that where you are?

Are you – wherever you are – there by your own will?

You could have gone on to heaven, but you stayed behind.

Isn't this a tremendous sacrifice for you? Why would you do it? Because I *asked* you to stay?

So now what happens to you?

An expert once told me these souls await reincarnation. Some of them, anyhow. Father Paul would probably agree. Weird old coot.

With Bluebonnets

Mary Ellen Barnes is the chief player in a taut biodrama that has been going on in Helen's uterus for nine months. Once every twenty-eight days, ever since her menarche, Helen's pituitary has urged her uterus to contract and reject incompatible objects; hence her periods. However, for the past nine months her corpus luteum has countermanded the rejection order: "Not yet! Not yet!" But then, two weeks short of nine months, the corpus luteum begins to degenerate. It loses control. Aha! cries the uterus. "I'm free! Free! I can finally get rid of this – *thing!*" And *pow!* The moment comes. At thirty-minute intervals, the uterine muscles begin to contract . . .

The baby's birthday will certainly be easy to remember: the first day of the D.C. Bar exam. To sort of sum it up, a hell of a time was had by all. Everything ran together. The afternoon before the exam, Helen started labor (we thought). I called a cab, and we got her out to Garfield. False labor, they said. They called Rothman, our OB. Leave her there, he said. It's time anyhow. We'll take the baby tomorrow.

"Go home," Helen insisted. "You've got to be bright and fresh for the exam tomorrow. Don't worry about me. I won't run away." She was right, of course. We held sweaty hands for a moment. Then I kissed her goodbye and returned to the apartment.

So, on the night before the exam, Helen was like on another planet and I was sitting at our little dinner table staring off into space. I couldn't think straight. I was having dark premonitions.

And now I did a weird thing. I am an agnostic. I haven't said a prayer since I was a kid in Sunday School. But now I remembered how Helen's mother had had miscarriages. Some genetic lung problem. I got down on my knees in our little kitchen, and I concentrated. Cybele (I thought), I know you're out there. Helen needs you. Help her have a healthy baby. Cybele, please stay with Helen tonight.

I got up. My knees hurt. I had done all I could. The matter was now up to powers far greater than mine.

And so back to the bar exam. It would start tomorrow morning with Civil Procedure. If I could just answer that first question in Civil Pro, I knew I could pass.

I went into our little living room and sat at the table with my books and notes and fiddled with the pages in my Civil Pro text. But it was no use. I was groggy. Maybe a nap would help. Just an hour. It was seven in the evening. I went into the bedroom and dropped crosswise across the bed.

I awoke, startled. I thought I had heard a lion roar. I sat up in bed. That's dumb, I thought. The zoo is way out in Rock Creek Park, five miles away. And in all the years we've lived here, we've never heard a peep out of the zoo.

I sat there and listened. No more lion. Just the regular reassuring street noises. Okay. It was all in my head. Nerves. About what you'd expect, with the baby and the exam both due tomorrow. I looked at the clock. Eight p.m. The fall equinox was approaching. It was still fairly light out. I got up, went to the bathroom, came back into the bedroom. I stuck my head out the window. Seven floors below, the White Tower was doing a good supper business.

Just then I heard the lion again. Exactly like old Numa, back in Forest Park in Fort West. I put my hands to my ears, and I thought, oh God! this is no time to start hallucinating.

And just then something flew in the window. I whirled around, startled. It circled the room . . . as though it was *searching?* It was big enough to be a sparrow . . . or a bat. I had a bizarre thought: Poe's raven? "Tell me what thy lordly name is on the Night's Plutonian Shore!" But I knew it was none of those. I knew what it was – a great noctuid moth, a Black Witch, with a six-inch wing span.

I watched it in open-mouthed paralysis.

Very daintily, after a couple of trial passes, it lit on a little cedar box on the chest of drawers. Then it turned, with the wings rising and falling slowly and gracefully, and it looked at me. Yes, in the semi-dark its eyes shone at me.

Then it leaped up into the air and vanished through the window. I ran after it and looked out, but couldn't see it.

Cybele, I thought.

I turned back to the little cedar box. There was only one thing in it. Helen chided me for keeping it, but I knew I could never part with it. I opened it and took out the little sheaf of stapled library slips that I had forged with Cybele's name, way back at JimBowie High, and which Diana Mulligan had sent with Cybele's posthumous wedding gift. Whatever she was trying to tell me had to be somewhere in this little packet. With trembling fingers I flipped through the papers one by one. When I came to the last one I noted once more that mysterious equation:

$$CoCl_2 \cdot 6H_2O \rightarrow CoCl_2 + 6H_2O$$
$$\text{Heat}$$

It was in her handwriting, of course. But what was she trying to tell me?

As I held the paper I felt something odd. A part of the paper seemed different, as though it had once been wet, and then had dried. I held it up to the light. Yes, something was different. Cybele, did you do this? Did you spill something on it fifteen years ago?

I was thinking back, back, back . . . long ago . . . in her class. (And I knew now that something was guiding my thoughts.) At school the plaster ceiling over the demonstration bench had leaked. That had sparked her lecture on hydrated salts. Plaster was hydrated calcium sulfate. Concrete was a hydration product. Lots of salts changed color when hydrated.

I ran into the kitchen and turned on the front burner. Very very carefully I held that last odd library pass high over the flame, and I held my breath as something began to take shape on the web of the paper. A couple of things, really. The first thing I noted: in the center was the imprint of lips – her lips, of course. In cobalt blue.

I'm not sure what I did in the next couple of minutes. I remember calling her name, and kissing that imprint. I remember choking, and my chest heaving, and tears filling my eyes.

Back in the living room I finally dried my eyes and got it all together. Cobalt chloride, $CoCl_2$, is almost colorless in dilute solution. It dries as the hydrate, $CoCl_2 \cdot 6H_2O$. When warmed, the hydrate loses water and the anhydrous salt turns blue. It makes a fine invisible ink. You develop it with heat.

But that wasn't all. There was that other thing. I studied the signature. It wasn't the same one I had so laboriously forged so long ago. "Wilson" was still there, but "Cybele" was gone. In its place was a word, a name. The whole thing now read, "Sibbach v Wilson." It was now a legal citation.

I should have been stunned. Or at least astonished. But no. I was beyond that. So she could change the molecules around. Very interesting. What else could my angel do?

No time to speculate. Back to the business at hand. She was telling me something. I remembered . . . there was a case . . . Sibbach . . . Supreme Court slip opinion . . . too late for the books. Did I make a note? I searched my papers. Nothing there. I'll bet the prof discussed it on the night I cut class to work on strontium. Damn.

The G.W. Law Library was two blocks down G Street. I was there in two minutes. And I found the case, *Sibbach* v *Wilson,* U.S. Supreme Court, 1941. My hands trembled as I read the eight pages of the opinion. Plaintiff, suing for injuries, couldn't be held in contempt for refusal to permit a physical examination.

Next morning at seven I called the hospital. No baby yet. No change. No nothing. I hurried on downtown to the Exam Building on F Street. The monitor handed out the papers.

Question Number One on Civil Pro asked, "Can plaintiff, suing for injuries, be held in contempt for refusal to permit a physical examination?"

(Now there's an interesting little epilog to this one. Some days later, when I was putting the library slips back in the little cedar box, I examined the last one very carefully. "Sibbach" was now back to "Cybele.")

We had an hour for lunch, then back to the exam rooms. I wasn't hungry. I got to a phone.

They couldn't tell me much. "She's in delivery."

"She's having the baby?"

"Probably not just yet."

What did *that* mean? I returned to the exam room.

At the end of the afternoon session I called the hospital again. I had a daughter. She and her mother were doing fine. I grabbed a cab and got out there fast.

On my way to the maternity ward I passed the hospital chapel. This was a somber room, neither large nor small, heavily carpeted, with church-like pews, a dais, platforms for flowers, and an altar. At the moment the only illumination was through a varicolored stained-glass window, and the spectral beams seemed to come to a sort of three-dimensional focus above and around the altar. The effect was very beautiful, and I stopped for a moment just to take it all in.

The light changed. The window darkened, but there was still a sort of reddish light. I saw then something I must have missed when I first looked in. A man was standing behind the altar, looking straight at me. He was holding something, a cup. *The* Cup? A soft crimson radiance was flowing from it and lighting up the man's face from below.

He smiled at me.

I stared, then rubbed my eyes and blinked a couple of times.

"Lukey? What —"

But as I stared, the light changed again, and once more came in strongly through the window. The image faded, vanished. I shrugged and passed on down the hall. All an optical illusion. In my state of mind it wasn't too surprising.

Helen was groggy but happy. I bent over her bed and we hugged for a long time. She mumbled, "Have you seen her?"

"Next stop."

"They'll bring her to the window. Later on you can hold her."

"Sure."

She took a deep breath in jerks, like a series of gasps. "Do you smell that?"

"Yes." I knew *she* was nearby. I had known ever since I had entered the room.

She waited a while. "Bluebonnets?"

"Yes, bluebonnets."

"Like back home."

"Yes."

"Marvelous." She got the word out slowly.

"Yes."

"You don't sound surprised."

I didn't say anything.

She went on. "You had a good life in chemistry. Maybe she should study chemistry. Where would be the best school?"

Cybele, I thought, what are you up to? All of a sudden I had a lot to think about. I said, "That's a long way off. Maybe she doesn't want to be a chemist. Maybe she'll be a musician, or a writer, or a homemaker, a loving wife and mother."

"She'll be a chemist, and a great one. She'll make wonderful discoveries. Oh, Joe, we must be supportive."

"Yeah," I said vaguely. There was too much here to figure out all at once.

"Stanford? MIT? Harvard?"

"All good ones." (Cybele! Come out, come out, wherever you are!)

Just then we noticed that Dr. Rothman was motioning to me from the doorway. As I went out into the hall with him, he sniffed. "Strange odor. Flowers?"

"Lupinus subcarnosus," I said.

"Oh." He let it go. His mind was on something else. I couldn't decipher his expression. It was puzzled, grim, mystified. He led me around to the office they let him use and he got to the point immediately.

"Your wife had a hard labor. The baby – well –" He studied me as though trying to assess how I would respond. He started again. "The baby is fine. I assure you, nothing to be concerned about. Absolutely nothing."

"But –?" I knew something was wrong. "She –?" I was stammering, and I think I was turning pale.

"She was stillborn," he said evenly. "We lost a heart beat soon after your wife arrived here yesterday."

"You didn't mention . . ."

"No. Often, we can save the child. Pointless to frighten the mother prematurely. And she still doesn't know." He looked at me curiously, as though I might have an answer to something that was bothering him. "Are you a religious man, Mr. Barnes?"

"Not especially." (My kneecaps began to ache.)

"Something you ought to look into," he said vaguely. "We put the dead baby aside as required by the rules. We filled out the certificate, with cause of death, stillborn. She was dead, Mr. Barnes. No heartbeat, no respiration. Nothing. She had been dead fifteen, twenty minutes, and then the nurses swear they saw a sort of light floating over her. A red radiance, they said, hovering. Then it faded, and she, the baby, began to cry. Quite some excitement." He paused and watched my face. "Come over here."

He walked over to a side wall, where he turned on the light board. Two X-ray plates were stuck in the slits. He pointed. "We took this one immediately after birth. It confirms our diagnosis, why she couldn't breathe." He touched an area on the plate with his pen. "This is her thymus gland. It contributes to the immune system. Normally it sits behind the trachea. Here in this first plate it's greatly enlarged. In fact it completely surrounds the trachea. It has absorbed several cartilege rings in the trachea and squeezed it shut. Internal strangulation. Inoperable. She was dead, Mr. Barnes. Dead. And growing cold."

"But –"

He ignored me. "Here she is, an hour later. Look at this plate. The thymus has shrunk back to normal. The trachea is normal, completely clear and functioning. Respiration, heart beat, body temperature, all vitals normal. Same infant. We checked bracelet, footprints, blood type. There can be absolutely no doubt. None. We don't know what to call it. It isn't resuscitation. It isn't revival. It gets us . . . into . . . ." He stopped and sighed, as though not quite sure how to continue. He took a deep breath. "The Director has asked me to speak for him. Word is going to get around. You saw how the nurses looked at you. And there's a bit of a buzz in radiology." He looked up at me, almost pleading. "This hospital is certified as one of the ten best in the country, Mr. Barnes. Garfield got two proficiency awards last year. Miracles we don't need. Do you understand?"

I didn't understand everything just yet. Cybele, of course, maybe with help from Lukey. But what exactly had she done? How far had she gone? I said, "I – well – I *think* so."

"What we'd like, Mr. Barnes, would you please not discuss these events with anybody . . . reporters . . . friends . . . anybody."

I looked dubious. "Pretty hard to hide a birth, doc."

"You know what I mean, *supernatural* aspects . . . if any . . . Surely you can see what would happen. Another Lourdes, Fatima. Pilgrimages. Crowds. Garfield is a hospital, not a shrine. We couldn't handle it. Nor could you."

He had a point. "You haven't told Helen?"

"No, that's up to you."

"Okay, it's a deal." I could decide later what to tell Helen. If anything.

He looked vastly relieved. "Well then, that's fine." But he hesitated. I waited. Finally he said, "Do *you* have . . . any idea . . ."

My thoughts hereabouts were still a bit chaotic. I remembered that strange session with Father Paul back in Fort West. He had hinted at the power of the Cup to reincarnate. Was it possible? I thought of Poe's gothic tales about erudite women who died and were reincarnated as their daughters, or some such. Morella: "And when my spirit departs shall the child live – thy child and mine." And Ligeia, who dies, becomes Rowena, who becomes Ligeia again. Whom would this child look like at sixteen? Would she inherit that delicate scent of bluebonnets? Oh Cybele, Cybele . . . I took a long deep breath.

Did I have any idea? Yes indeed. It finally all came together. I knew exactly what had happened.

She had known it would unfold this way. How far back had she known? As far back as that night in Forest Park? Yes, at least that far. She had known I would be on that path. Or was it even farther back, in the cave, that afternoon by Sycamore Creek, and her encounter there with Father Paul – and me?

Had the mystic Prior foreseen the whole thing? Had he helped her design her life, starting there? He had said to me, "When the child comes, think of these moments." And she had known there would be a child. "Our child," she had said, as she lay dying.

She had tried to tell me. She had foretold everything: her coming death, the long wait in the wings, the dead baby, the baby's re-entry into life.

Had she used her magic lore of chemistry to enslave me? Not really. Well, maybe a little. Actually, though, I had succumbed to the wiles of Lady Chemia long before I met Cybele.

In the beginning I used to ask myself, why *me?* She was a beautiful, mature woman. I was a callow youth. She could have had *any* man. What could *I* give her that the others couldn't? Well, of course now we know. I could give her life after death.

Had she killed the baby and taken her body? The thought was ignoble; I dismissed it instantly.

Had she used me? Or technically, Helen and me? It looks that way. On the other hand she had given herself up to be used by us. It was an interlocking reciprocity, a perfect classic symbiosis.

But a very puzzled Dr. Rothman is waiting for my answer.

Did I have any idea?

I looked the good doctor straight in the eye. "I have no idea."

He smiled. "Well, that's it, I guess. Thought you ought to know. Come on, you'll want to look at her."

And so to the nursery. We went inside. I picked the baby up, and she and I looked at each other for a while. I studied her. She studied me. Oh, I knew that face, those marvelous expressive eyes (barely able yet to see), those lips, even now twisted into that happy wry grin (though newborns aren't supposed to be able to smile). How Cybele had done this, I do not know. All I knew was, this was her doing, and it was miraculous.

Rothman grinned and touched my sleeve.

"Gotta go." A nurse took the baby. I went back to Helen. I sat on the edge of her bed and we talked. About how healthy the baby was. (Helen said, proudly, "You should hear her holler!") About who she looked like. She would be tall.

And then she said, "Joe, they asked me what name to put on her birth record."

"You remembered 'Mary Ellen'?"

"Yeah, I did, but I was thinking funny, Joe, from the anesthesia, and all."

I got a grip on myself.

She continued. "It came to me, Joe, almost like in a dream. I couldn't get it out of my head. It was exactly right for her. An absolutely beautiful name." She was fingering Father Paul's golden leaf, pinned to her bed jacket.

I took a long deep breath, let it out slowly. "Yeah?"

"Sybyl," she said. "S-Y-B-Y-L. Sybyl Barnes. What do you think?"

Think? I was thinking of the little New Testament, held open by the withered fingers of my dead first wife. Matthew 28:20. "Lo, I am with you always." She could have gone on to her heaven, to her own personal well-deserved rapture; but she had chosen this. This was love beyond love. No matter how you spelled it, it had a name: Cybele.

What happens now to this incredible *ménage à trois?* How would it be from here on in? I decided I really didn't care. Only one thing mattered: our child was dead, and now lives.

"Well?" demanded Helen, "what do you think?"

"Sybyl is a very beautiful name," I said. "Sybyl E., with bluebonnets."

THE NEW ENGLAND
SCIENCE FICTION ASSOCIATION (NESFA)
AND NESFA PRESS

Recent books from NESFA Press:

- *Rings* by Charles L. Harness $25
- *An Ornament to His Profession* by Charles L. Harness $25
- *Entities* by Eric Frank Russell $29
- *Major Ingredients* by Eric Frank Russell $29
- *Dimensions of Sheckley* by Robert Sheckley $29
- *From These Ashes* by Fredric Brown $29
- *The Compleat Boucher* by Anthony Boucher $25
- *First Contacts: The Essential Murray Leinster* $27
- *His Share of Glory* by C. M. Kornbluth $27
- *The Best of James H. Schmitz* by James H. Schmitz $22

The Complete SF of William Tenn
- *Immodest Proposals* (Vol. 1) $29
- *Here Comes Civilization* (Vol. 2) $29

The Essential Hal Clement:
- *Trio for Slide Rule & Typewriter* (Vol. 1) $25
- *Music of Many Spheres* (Vol. 2) $25
- *Variations on a Theme by Sir Isaac Newton* (Vol. 3) $25

Details and many more books available online at: www.nesfa.org/press

Books may be ordered by writing to:
NESFA Press
PO Box 809
Framingham, MA 01701

We accept checks, Visa, or MasterCard. Please add $3 postage and handling per order.

The New England Science Fiction Association:

NESFA is an all-volunteer, non-profit organization of science fiction and fantasy fans. Besides publishing, our activities include running Boskone (New England's oldest SF convention) in February each year, producing a semi-monthly newsletter, holding discussion groups relating to the field, and hosting a variety of social events. If you are interested in learning more about us, we'd like to hear from you. Write to our address above!

Acknowledgments

Thanks for Michael Walsh (and the partial grant from Old Earth Books), and the crew of Bryan Cholfin, Erica Ginter, and Colleen Cahill who did the initial work.

To George Flynn—NESFA's own Quality Control (who finally had something to do in the Spring, tra la!).

To George Zebrowski for continued advice, work, and essential support services

To Mark Olson (for being computer support and printer liaison— among other things, of course.)

And to Iodine-131.

— Priscilla Olson
June, 2002